He'd read the *Who's Who* of the wedding party guests in his room, seen a Sally on the list and thought of her, as he always did if he saw her name, but never in his wildest imaginings had he dreamt it would be *his* Sally.

'No. She's not your Sally. She's David's,' he reminded himself sharply, and felt a stab of something that could only be jealousy. Crazy. He'd blown any chance of happiness with her when he'd married Clare. He had no right to be jealous.

He strode on, following a path around the hotel and behind the lawned terrace at the back. Running away, he told himself in disgust. He knew exactly what he was doing. But, whether he liked it or not, in a few minutes he had to go back in there, put on a cheerful wedding face and pretend to enjoy himself, when all he wanted to do was get in the car and leave.

'Liar,' he growled. 'You want to talk to her, to get her alone and find out how she is, touch her, hear her voice again, get to know the woman she is now. And if you're really lucky, you'll be utterly indifferent to her.'

He gave a snort of disbelief. Not a chance.

Dear Reader

I never meant to write my previous book,
A WIFE AND CHILD TO CHERISH. My husband
and I went to a truly wonderful wedding, of very
dear friends, and it was so inspirational I came home
and immediately started to write a story. It was about
old flames who meet again at the wedding of mutual
friends—except I couldn't get it off the ground,
because I didn't know the couple who were getting
married, and in the very earliest paragraphs Sally, the
heroine of the book I'd started, said to the bride and
groom, 'I'm so happy for you, after all you've been
through'—or words to that effect. Hmm. So what *had*
the happy couple been through? And how did they
meet? And why is this wedding such a triumph for
them? I couldn't walk away from Patrick and Annie,
and I couldn't move on until I'd written their story first!

But, having written that prequel, here, finally,
is the story I always meant to write. The story of
Jack and Sally, who met ten years ago and whose
love was never resolved as circumstances found them
marrying other people. As they meet again they realise
that the love and passion they shared has never gone
away, and that it's the vital ingredient that has been
missing in both of their marriages. I hope you enjoy
HIS VERY OWN WIFE AND CHILD, which starts—
as you might have guessed—at a wedding!

Happy reading!

Best wishes

Caroline

HIS VERY OWN
WIFE AND CHILD

BY

CAROLINE ANDERSON

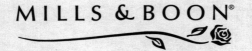

MILLS & BOON®

First published in Great Britain 2007
Harlequin Mills & Boon Limited,
Eton House, 18-24 Paradise Road, Richmond, Surrey TW9 1SR

© Caroline Anderson 2007

ISBN-13: 978 0 263 85230 1
ISBN-10:   0 263 85230 X

Set in Times Roman 10½ on 12½ pt
03-0407-49563

Printed and bound in Spain
by Litografia Rosés, S.A., Barcelona

Caroline Anderson has the mind of a butterfly. She's been a nurse, a secretary, a teacher, run her own soft-furnishing business, and now she's settled on writing. She says, 'I was looking for that elusive something. I finally realised it was variety, and now I have it in abundance. Every book brings new horizons and new friends, and in between books I have learned to be a juggler. My teacher husband John and I have two beautiful and talented daughters, Sarah and Hannah, umpteen pets, and several acres of Suffolk that nature tries to reclaim every time we turn our backs!' Caroline also writes for the Mills & Boon® Romance series.

Recent titles by the same author:

*A WIFE AND CHILD TO CHERISH
  (Medical Romance™)
MATERNAL INSTINCT
  (Medical Romance™)
THE BABY FROM NOWHERE
  (Medical Romance™)
ASSIGNMENT: CHRISTMAS
  (Medical Romance™)
THE PREGNANT TYCOON (Romance)

The Audley mini-series

CHAPTER ONE

IT COULDN'T be him.

Not here. She was seeing things.

'Oh, Sally, it's so good to see you!' Annie hugged her hard, then threw a sparkling smile at the others. 'Hi, David, hi, boys. Welcome back. Come on in!'

She had no choice. Annie was towing her into the hotel, arm still round her shoulders, and David was behind her with the boys, so there was nothing she could do but allow herself to be carried along. And, anyway, he couldn't be here. The whole of the little country house hotel was booked for the wedding, and she'd seen the guest list. There was no way she would have missed his name. She was just fantasising—tired, emotional, with all this love in the air...

'Are you all right? At least none of you seem to have broken anything! Good journey back from the airport?'

Sally found a smile. 'Yes, we're fine, no fractures and the road was clear. We've made really good time.' She put the man out of her mind and concentrated on Annie, hugging her again and then holding her at arm's length to study her. 'Anyway, never mind us, how are you? You're the one getting married tomorrow and I wasn't even here to help you with the last-minute things. Fine matron of honour I am! I feel so guilty, and if it hadn't been booked already there's no way I would have abandoned you like that just to go skiing. Did you get everything done? Are you coping?'

Annie laughed, her face radiant. 'Don't worry about me, I've never been better. I can't wait, and Patrick's been brilliant, so you can relax. You know, I really didn't have a clue what happiness was until I met him, but he's just…' She trailed off, shrugging and laughing off the emotion that had visibly bubbled to the surface.

'I'm so glad for you,' Sally said fervently, hugging her yet again and blinking away her own tears. 'You deserve to be happy. You've been through hell. I'm really glad it's over and things are looking so great for you all.'

'Me, too.' Annie's hug tightened for a moment, then she released Sally and took a step back. 'Look, I'm up to my eyes a bit for the next few minutes, sorting out a problem with the food, so why don't you check in and sort yourselves out, then come down and find us when you're ready? Patrick and Katie are downstairs in the dungeons with the others, and I should be there soon.'

'Dungeons?' That was Ben, bouncing up beside her and staring at Annie wide-eyed. 'Really?'

Annie nodded seriously. 'Well, they used to be, I think. It's a very old house, and I think they kept prisoners downstairs at one time—smugglers, probably! There's a little room with an iron grille instead of a door, and there are iron rings on the wall to tie people up to.' She grinned as she walked away. 'You'd better be good or you might end up in there!'

Ben's eyes widened even further. 'Cool!' he said, and

whirled round to tell his elder brother, just as Alex took a step forward.

There was a sickening crunch, Ben yelped, Alex buried his nose in his hands and howled, 'Ow!' As the blood started to drip through his fingers, David sighed, put down the cases and rummaged in his pockets.

'Sally, have you got a—?'

'Allow me,' a voice said, and Sally straightened up and felt the air whoosh from her lungs. It couldn't be, it really couldn't—

'Hello, Sal.'

She didn't even notice the box of tissues he was holding out. She was too busy trying to stay upright. Her heart was pounding so hard she couldn't hear, and it was jammed in her throat, totally obstructing her airway so that she had to make a conscious effort to drag in a breath, then another.

'Cheers,' David said, grabbing the tissues and shoving a handful at Alex. 'Here. You're dripping on the floor. Sally, are you OK? You look as if you've seen a ghost.'

She felt a bubble of hysterical laughter. A ghost? Or just her biggest ever mistake come back to haunt her? She shook her head, partly to clear it. 'I'm fine, just a bit light-headed. It must be jet-lag,' she said, turning her attention belatedly to Alex.

Oh, lord. Alex!

Alex, for all sorts of reasons—but the most pressing one was the spreading stain on the hotel carpet. The rest could wait. Please, God.

She stared at the clump of bloody tissues and the mess on the floor. She should be dealing with it, with him, and all she could think about was the man who'd made her happier than she'd ever been in her life—and had then walked away without a backward glance, leaving her life in chaos. What was he *doing* here? Why…?

'Thank you,' she managed somehow, and dragging her eyes from his, she turned her attention to her son. 'Darling, let me see.'

'It's broken,' Alex mumbled round the tissues. 'He's smashed it to bits, I know he has.'

'Don't be melodramatic,' David said calmly. 'Let your mother look.' And he gently prised the boy's hands away from his face.

Alex yelped. 'Dad, careful! It's broken!'

'I don't think so,' Sally said, studying it and wondering if the blood would come out of the carpet or if the hotel would charge them for it. Thank God it was patterned, she thought inconsequentially, and then couldn't believe she was worrying about anything so trivial when—

'May I?' Jack said to Alex. 'I'm a doctor—I work in an emergency department, so I see this sort of thing all the time.' With Alex's wary nod, he ignored her murmur of dissent and bent his knees to bring himself down to Alex's level, and her heart went into hyperdrive.

Oh, lord. They were eye to eye, nose to nose…

'I'm Jack, by the way,' he said with a smile. And then he touched him. He ran his fingertip lightly over the bridge of Alex's nose, peered up it, then gave the cartilage an experimental little wiggle that brought a muted squawk of protest from her son. 'Sorry. I'm sure it must be sore, but the septum hasn't deviated—that's the bit in the middle between your nostrils—and it hasn't moved sideways, and it feels OK—'

'No, it doesn't!' Alex retorted, and Jack laughed not unkindly and straightened up.

'I'm sure it doesn't, but noses are very sensitive. They hurt like crazy when you bump them, even if you don't really damage them. If it's any consolation you'll probably have an impressive black eye in the morning, but I don't think you can sue your brother for anything more dramatic. It's not even really bleeding any longer.'

Alex grunted, and Jack handed him another tissue, took away the blood-soaked ones and held out his hand to David with the open smile that was his trade mark.

'Jack Logan,' he said. 'I'm an old friend of Patrick's. And you must be David Brown, Sally's husband, if the *Who's Who* I found in the room's to be believed. Sal and I worked together years ago, on one of my rotations.'

'Briefly,' she put in, and wondered if the edge in her voice was noticeable. Probably. And if he was an old friend of Patrick's, why hadn't his name come up?

'It's a small world,' David said, shaking his hand and returning his smile.

Sally wasn't smiling. She was beyond it, too shocked to function except on autopilot, because she'd loved him so much, had given him everything of herself, and just when she'd needed him...

'Mum, is Alex OK?'

She pulled herself together and looked down at Ben, hovering guiltily beside her and staring at his brother's nose with awe. She reached out and squeezed his shoulder.

'He's fine. Don't worry, darling. We need to check in and find our rooms, and I ought to do something about the carpet.'

'Leave the carpet to me. I'll get it sorted,' Jack said in that low, slightly gruff voice that made her blood heat and her heart jiggle.

Crazy. Insane! After all these years, she should have

been immune to his charms. She forced herself to meet his eyes. 'Thank you. I'll go and sort the kids out, make sure Alex is OK. We'll see you later.'

Emphasis on the 'we', please note. Happily married woman, with two children and a safe, sensible career as a senior A and E nurse. So frightfully normal it was almost a cliché. And she had no business letting her eyes rest longingly on his features, noting the new touch of grey threaded through his toffee-coloured hair, the silver mingling with the gold streaks at his temples. That summer, too, his hair had faded to gold in the sun, and she guessed he'd been somewhere hot just recently. Either that or he'd had it highlighted, and she couldn't imagine him having either the patience or the vanity for that.

He had crow's feet now round those fabulous slate-blue eyes, she noticed, made all the more obvious by his tan. She'd always known he'd get them, because he'd laughed all the time, and the brackets around his mouth had deepened, too.

Oh, that mouth. Her eyes dropped lower, checking out those firm, sculptured lips she'd known so well. She shouldn't be wondering if they would still feel the same, if he'd taste the same, if his hands were still so clever…

'I'll look forward to it,' he murmured, and for a hideously embarrassing second she thought she'd voiced her feelings out loud, but no. He was just answering her 'See you later' with another stock response. Relief—and something else—sent her blood surging through her veins and her heart off once more on that wild-goose chase, and she struggled for a smile.

Dragging her eyes from his face, she ushered the children towards the reception desk where David was already checking them in, and by the time they'd filled in the registration form there was a member of the hotel staff cheerfully sorting out the carpet and Jack was nowhere to be seen.

Good, she told herself, and wondered why it didn't feel good, why it felt as if the sun had gone behind a cloud and all the warmth had drained from the day...

He couldn't believe she was here. He'd read the *Who's Who* of the wedding party guests in his room, seen a Sally on the list and thought of her as he always did if he saw her name, but never in his wildest imaginings had he dreamt it would be *his* Sally.

'No. She's not your Sally. She's David's,' he reminded himself sharply, and felt a stab of something that could only be jealousy. Crazy. He'd blown any chance of happiness with her when he'd married Clare. He had no right to be jealous of David.

He strode on, following a path around the hotel and behind the lawned terrace at the back, down into the woodland below. Running away, he told himself in disgust. He knew exactly what he was doing, and he knew why, but it didn't make it sensible because, whether he liked it or not, in a few minutes he had to go back in there, put on a cheerful wedding face and pretend to enjoy himself, when all he wanted to do was get in the car and leave.

'Liar,' he growled. 'You want to talk to her, to get her alone and find out how she is, touch her, hear her voice again, get to know the woman she is now. And if you're really lucky, you'll be utterly indifferent to her.'

He gave a snort of disbelief. Not a chance. When he'd seen her in the entrance hall, he'd felt as if he'd been hit by a truck. There was no way he'd be indifferent to Sally until he was dead. The best he could hope for in the next two days was a little dignity. With a sigh of resignation, he turned and made his way back to the hotel.

'Jack seems a nice man.'

Nice? Jack? Not in a million years. Sexy, yes—fascinating, absolutely. But nice? She made a noncommittal 'mmm' noise and carried on unpacking.

'You worked with him, he said?'

Sally hung up her dress, tugged at a crease and picked up a pair of trousers, threading them onto the hanger with exaggerated care. 'Very briefly. It was years and years ago. He was an SHO on my new ward, but he was due to finish. We only coincided by a few weeks.' Amazing weeks. Weeks that had changed her life…

'You must have made an impression. He seems to remember you quite clearly.'

'It's my sparkling personality,' she said, flashing him a smile and wishing he'd let it drop. The last thing she wanted to do was get into a conversation about Jack Logan with a man she'd spent the last nine years regretting marrying—and where had *that* come from?

The trousers fell from her fingers, and she bent and picked them up and brushed them absently. Really? She regretted it? But she'd got the boys, and they'd had a good life together. Hadn't they? And what was the past tense all about?

'Nice touch.'

She glanced over and saw him flicking through the contents of a shallow little box that had been lying on the bed.

'*Who's Who* of the wedding party, schedule of events for tonight and tomorrow, even a map of the surroundings in case we want a walk. See.'

Halting her run-away thoughts, she crossed over to the bed and took the box, all the sheets inside beautifully decorated with a delicate motif and enclosed in a tissue folder. The outside of the box was decorated with tiny pressed rosebuds, and it brought a lump to her throat.

It was so unashamedly romantic, so absolutely perfect, and Annie's happiness shone through every word. They made a wonderful couple, and Sally felt a twinge of something that could have been jealousy. She squashed it hard. They *deserved* their happiness. She wasn't going to envy them it, they were more than welcome.

She touched the rosebuds wistfully. 'Pretty, isn't it? And thoughtful—typical Annie. She's been planning it for ages, but she hadn't finished when we went on holiday,' she said, and put the box down with hands that were suddenly unsteady.

Was he in the *Who's Who* now? He hadn't been—so he *must* be the missing friend that Patrick had been trying to locate, the man he'd called Oz. She remembered now that Jack had been born in Australia, but apart from the odd word if he was stressed—or aroused, and she wasn't going to let herself think about that!—you really wouldn't have known, and she'd forgotten until now.

Obviously, in the last couple of weeks while they'd been away, Patrick had tracked him down. Hence Jack's presence here now, turning her brain into mush and her body into a wildfire.

How was she going to cope with seeing Jack over the next few days? David wasn't stupid. He'd be bound to notice if her behaviour was different, and there was no way it wouldn't be. For a start, the moment she'd seen him she'd stopped breathing, and David had picked up on it instantly. If she looked as if she'd seen a ghost every time she set eyes on him, it was going to be a dead give-away, and she couldn't bear to hurt David by making him think she was still in love with Jack. He'd been so good to her—

'Look, Mum! I'm getting a black eye!'

Alex and Ben burst into the room, Alex's pain forgotten in favour of pride in his wound, and she examined it dutifully and made admiring noises. In fact, it was just the merest touch of purple extending into his lower eyelid from the corner of his left eye, but by the morning it might be more impressive, and she had the feeling that Alex wouldn't mind that at all!

'Come on, we ought to be going down,' David said, checking his tie in the mirror and running an assessing eye over the boys. 'Are you all set?'

They nodded, and he turned to Sally. 'Are you ready?'

She shook her head. 'Give me five minutes. Why don't you take the boys down and introduce them to the others? I'll be down soon.'

'OK. Don't be long.'

He took the boys out. She could hear them chattering excitedly on the way down the corridor, David's deeper voice steadying them and warning Ben to mind the step.

Then a door swung shut and silence descended, broken only by the beat of her heart.

She closed her eyes and rested her cheek against the cool glass of the mirror. She wasn't ready for this. She'd had no warning, no time to prepare herself either physically or mentally.

She'd put on weight, her hair needed a really good cut instead of the quick trim that was all she had time to fit in these days, and...

'What are you think about?' she asked herself, straightening up and glaring sternly at her reflection in the mirror. 'You're married—so's he. There are more important things to worry about. It doesn't matter what you look like!'

But it did, for her pride if nothing else, and she searched her face for the changes he'd find. Tiny lines, of tiredness and worry and the stress of her job, and the other day she'd even found a grey hair. At thirty-two? She'd yanked it out, but she doubted Clare would have a grey hair or a wrinkle.

Of course she'd only ever met her once before, so it would be interesting—was that the word?—to see her now. She might have run to seed, if there was any justice, but she'd have to be going some to look worse than this.

She dropped her eyes to her waist, sucked in her stomach and turned sideways, then sighed. The best underwear in the world wouldn't take away the fact that she'd put on a stone and lost the pert youthfulness she'd had all those years ago, she thought, and then hauled herself up short again.

So what? She had two beautiful children to show for it, and a husband who loved her, a comfortable home and a job she was proud of. She didn't need him, in any way, shape or form, and it didn't matter to her in the slightest what he thought of her or what Clare looked like. He was the one who'd walked away, and there was no way on God's green earth she wanted him back.

At all.

Ever.

She yanked herself up straight, gave herself a stern nod in the mirror and went out of the door. She could do this. She could…

* * *

She looked wonderful.

Softer, somehow, as if the years had mellowed her. She'd gained a little weight, and it suited her. She looked tired, though, and there were shadows in her eyes that had nothing to do with working too hard. They always used to sparkle, he mused. Except on that day—the day Clare had erupted into their lives, the day he'd walked away.

He swallowed and turned back to Patrick, forcing himself to pay attention. His old friend was getting married tomorrow, to a woman who lit up his world, and all Jack had to do was listen to him talk about her and try not to wonder what his own life would have been like if Clare hadn't come back into it…

Funny, how that touch of grey didn't age him, although compared to Patrick's prematurely grey hair it was unnoticeable, and it had certainly done Patrick's looks no harm at all. No, the silver threads at Jack's temples suited him somehow—gave him a little of the gravitas that he sorely needed to counteract those laughing eyes. And it tied in with the crow's feet round his eyes and the laughter lines that bracketed his mouth. He'd always laughed a lot, she remembered—made her laugh, too, but that had been years ago.

Nearly ten, to be exact, when she'd been only twenty-three and in her first staff job in the hospital where he'd been working as an SHO. He was four years older than her—he'd taken a gap year before uni and by the sound of it had blagged his way around the world with an ancient backpack and enough charm to sink a battleship. She could easily believe it. There'd been no lack of that charm in the man she'd met and fallen for. He must be thirty-six now, if not thirty-seven, she thought in astonishment. Where on earth had their lives gone?

He was standing by the bar with Patrick, and as she hesitated in the doorway, he threw back his head and laughed at something Patrick had said, then turned and caught sight of her. She was staring at him, arrested by that wonderful sound that she'd never thought to hear again, and there wasn't time to look away.

His laughter ebbed, and with a quick murmured word to Patrick, he excused himself and crossed the room.

'Sal.'

That was all. One word and her heart turned upside down.

'So where's Clare?' she asked, getting it over with as quickly as possible, and for a second he looked startled.

'Clare? She's at home. In New Zealand.'

So far away. She felt a stupid pang of loss. She'd often wondered where he was, tried to picture him, wondered if they'd run into each other—hoped...

'And your children?' she asked, turning the knife another time, but not just in herself, it seemed, because something happened to his eyes.

'There was only Chloe,' he said. 'I don't see as much of her as I'd like.'

There was a wealth of sadness in those few words, and a story behind them, she'd stake her life on it. But she didn't want to know. She really didn't. And it seemed he didn't want her to, because he said no more, just smiled and shrugged, and she had a crazy urge to take him in her arms and comfort him. No. Madness. He was married, and so was she. If she kept saying it, maybe she'd remember.

'So how long are you here? Just for the wedding, or are you hoping to snatch a little longer?'

'Trying to get rid of me already?' he murmured with a crooked grin, then shook his head. 'I've taken a six-month sabbatical—that's why Patrick had trouble getting hold of me. I've been travelling. I'm here for a few weeks, dog-sitting for them while they're away and catching up when they get back, getting a look at the area maybe, and then I'm off travelling again. You know me,' he said lightly. 'Always something else to see. So what about you? Have you had to come far today?'

She shook her head, wondering what Clare thought of his wanderlust. And he'd had the gall to have her feeling sorry for him because he didn't see enough of his daughter? He should try being at home, then! 'No. Well, yes, we've just been skiing in Canada and we came straight from the airport, but I'm working locally. I work in the same hospital as Annie and Patrick. So what are you doing? You said something about being an ED doctor?'

He nodded. 'Yes. Suicidal career move, really, because there's not much call for private work to boost the coffers,' he said with a wry grin, 'but it just appealed. When you see people all mashed up and you can sort them out and give them another chance at life—that's amazing. And it got addictive, so I ended up working for MSF for a while— Médecins Sans Frontières—getting stuck into all sorts of nasty natural and manmade disasters.' He laughed and ran a hand through his hair. 'Still, that's all history now and I've grown up. So what about you? Are you a paper-pushing hot-shot manager yet?'

She shook her head. 'That's not my style. I'm strictly clinical, a proper hands-on nurse,' she told him. 'Actually I like it—prefer it to a more administrative role—but even if I hadn't, maternity leave rather scuppered my career progress.'

His grin was wry. 'I can imagine. So what about David? What does he do? He looks like a civil engineer or an accountant or something.'

Oh, lord, he was so close to the truth it was painful.

'He's a structural engineer,' she confessed, and he threw back his head and laughed again.

'I knew it!' he teased. 'Middle England. You always were destined for it.'

And we're very happy, she reminded herself, and I have no business looking at you like this, as if I'm trying to memorise every line on your face, every shadow, every hair, every tiny subtlety of expression...

'We meet again.'

He looked past her, still smiling. 'David. Hi. Sal was just telling me all about you,' he said, and then smiled down at Alex in a way that made her heart hitch against her ribs. 'Hello again, young man. How's the nose?'

'OK. I've got a black eye, though—sort of.'

'I can see. Impressive.'

Alex wrinkled his nose and then winced. 'Not very impressive yet,' he said disgustedly.

'Ah, well, it might be better in the morning. It's usually more spectacular the second day.' He turned to Ben and grinned. 'And how's the other wounded soldier? Sore head?'

'I've got a bump—feel!' he instructed proudly, taking Jack's hand and placing it on his hair.

Sally watched, spellbound, as his gentle fingers searched out the bump and measured it with due solemnity. 'Excellent. I'm impressed with you both.'

Ben beamed, and Sally felt her heart hitch again as Jack smiled down at her boys. If only...

Oh, damn, she was going to cry, and she absolutely never cried. She had to get them away.

'Jack, you'll have to excuse us, we need to talk to Annie. We've only just got back from our holiday and I should have been helping her. And, anyway, we can't monopolise you—Patrick's looking lonely and you've come a long way to see him.'

And she whisked her family away, crushing the longing to stay there and talk to him all evening. Too dangerous, for all sorts of reasons. Nearly ten years clearly hadn't been long enough to neutralise her feelings, and if she stood there any longer she was just going to disgrace herself. Beg him to run his fingers through *her* hair, feel *her* scalp, knead it with those gentle, clever fingers that were so diabolically good at touching her until she begged for more...

No. Stop it. You're here for Annie. Everything else can wait.

CHAPTER TWO

THE day of the wedding dawned bright and clear.

David was up and off at seven, playing golf with the other men, and Sally had a lazy morning ahead of her. The children were all sorted, a hands-on falconry experience lined up for them at ten, and all she had to do was get ready for the wedding at three. Annie was with the hairdresser until eleven-thirty, and since her own hair couldn't hold a kink and simply needed washing and drying, she was free.

She'd done her nails yesterday, passing the time on the flight, and all she had to do before the wedding was have a quick shower. Their clothes had been left with Annie rather than taken to Canada, and she ought to check just to make sure there weren't creased, but she'd had a quick look the previous night and they'd seemed fine. And there was nothing else that needed her attention, and nothing that involved seeing Jack, thank goodness, because he would be playing golf with the others. So she had time on her hands.

She should have felt relaxed, but she didn't. Instead, she felt tense and wired and restless, and it got worse as the morning went on. She and the boys had a late breakfast and then she took them down to the falconry display and watched for a few minutes, then left them to it. They were enthralled, and didn't need her hovering over them like a mother hen. They already knew all the other children there, and they were having a fantastic time, so she had the rest of the morning to herself.

So, what to do with it?

She paused at the bottom of the stairs. She'd meant to check over their clothes now, but instead she found herself drawn back to the dungeons. It was cosy and peaceful down there, a tranquil little hide-away, and she ordered a pot of coffee and settled down in the little room with the iron grille for a door to flick through a magazine and relax for a few minutes.

'Coffee, madam,' a low, soft voice murmured, and she looked up, startled, straight into Jack's smiling eyes.

Oh, lord, she was going to whimper out loud if he kept on looking at her like that...

'I thought you were playing golf?' she said accusingly, willing her heart to slow.

'No. Didn't fancy it. Always thought it was a fairly pointless game really, whacking little balls round in circles, and, besides, I thought it might give us time to catch up.'

She sucked in a breath. No. He wasn't going to do this to her again.

'What makes you think we need to catch up?' she asked stiffly, and he threw her a crooked little smile and handed her a coffee from the tray—set for two, she noticed. Damn. What was he doing? She took it, her hand shaking so much she slopped it in the saucer.

'Maybe what I meant was that I wanted time to talk to you—to explain, to apologise,' he said quietly.

She blotted coffee. 'For walking out on me ten years

ago? Hardly necessary. In case you haven't noticed, I've moved on.'

'Oh, I've noticed. I've also noticed the shadows in your eyes, and the way the light dies in them when you aren't putting on your face.'

'What face?' she snapped, gulping down a mouthful of coffee and burning her tongue. She was going to have to give up drinking it. It was nothing but trouble.

'The face that tells the world you're all right, that you're happy.'

'I *am* happy,' she said fiercely.

'Are you? Lucky you.'

Her heart lurched and she reminded herself about his wanderlust. 'Maybe you'd be happier if you spent more time with your family,' she said with a touch of acid, but he just gave a wry, slightly bitter chuckle and shook his head.

'I don't think so.' His smile was crooked and tugged at her heartstrings, and that look was back in his eyes. 'Do I really have to explain to you, of all people, about the intricacies of a loveless marriage?'

It took her breath away. How had he seen? 'My marriage isn't loveless,' she said defensively, when she could speak again.

'No?' His mouth kicked up in a gentle smile. 'Forgive me, I must have been mistaken. But Clare and I should never have married.'

Oh, hell. He was going to do the 'poor misunderstood me' line and she'd fall for it, she knew she would. Well, she wouldn't. She just wouldn't. She was married, and so was he, and if she had to say it on the hour every hour for the next two days, so be it. But to know he'd been unhappy all this time...

'You know I wouldn't have had an affair with you if I hadn't believed that my relationship with her was over,' he said softly. 'But the baby changed everything.'

She swallowed. Oh, yes. 'They have a habit of doing that,' she said, and put her cup down before she could do any more damage. 'I have to go. I'm Annie's matron of honour, and I've only seen her for a few minutes this morning. I need to help her.'

'We'll meet again later, then—for the wedding. I'm Patrick's best man.'

Of course. And she was matron of honour. And as such, they'd be thrown together. She closed her eyes briefly, then stood up. 'Then you'll have things to do—speeches to write and so on. I'll see you later.'

And if she was really lucky, she'd get through it without making a fool of herself every time he looked at her…

'Are you OK? You looked as if you'd seen a ghost last night.'

Again? She found a smile for Annie, who even on her wedding day was worrying about other people. 'Just jet-lag,' she lied, and checked the bride's dress again. 'Turn round, the back isn't lying quite right,' she said, avoiding Annie's all-too-seeing eyes. She tweaked the lacing on the basque unnecessarily, then stepped back. 'Let me see you now.'

Annie did a little twirl, the soft old gold of the silk echoing the highlights in her hair. Not white or ivory, she'd insisted, because she didn't want to bring back echoes of Patrick's first tragic wedding, but gold, mellow and understated and utterly perfect with her colouring.

Sally sighed. 'That colour's fabulous on you. You're so lucky to be able to wear it. I'd look as if I'd crawled through mud.'

'No, you wouldn't, but that lovely soft wine red would drown me completely. It needs your dark hair to set it off—and the cut's fabulous with your curvy figure.'

Sally glanced in the mirror and tugged at the bodice. It was revealing altogether too much of her pale, milky skin for her liking. It had been years since her cleavage had had an airing, and she hadn't worried about it until Jack had shown up. And now… She tugged again fruitlessly and gave up. 'Curvy? Try fat.'

'You're not fat, you're beautiful. Womanly. I've always envied you your curves.'

'Eat more chocolate,' she advised, and gave Annie's dress another little tweak. 'Oh, you look absolutely stunning—radiant—and so do you, Katie,' she said, studying Annie's little princess in softest pink. 'Gorgeous. Wait till Patrick sees you both. He'll be so proud.'

Annie smiled a little nervously. 'Good. I'd hate to let him down.'

Sally hugged her carefully, and blinked away the tears. 'Not a chance. Come on, it's time to go down and start the rest of your life.'

And all she had to do was point Katie in the right direction and ignore Jack for the rest of the day.

How hard could it possibly be?

The wedding was beautiful.

It was a very simple ceremony, in the company of their dearest and closest friends and family, but hugely significant to both of them. In very different ways they'd both had tragic marriages, and to take this step must have taken unbelievable courage, but there they were, standing side by side in front of all their friends, about to take this huge leap of faith again.

If they'd been apprehensive, Sally wouldn't have been at all surprised, but there was no uncertainty, no hesitation in the way Patrick held out his hand and Annie placed hers in it and went up on tiptoe to kiss his cheek, the joy shining from her eyes. From her vantage point behind Annie and Patrick, Sally could feel the love radiating off them both, see the joy and pride in their eyes, the total absence of any doubt.

The registrar asked, 'Who gives this woman to be married to this man?'

And when eight-year-old Katie replied, 'I do,' there wasn't a dry eye in the house.

They were seated together, of course.

It could have been a great deal worse. As matron of honour and best man, they could have been on a formal top table, but because it was Patrick and Annie, because they wanted the whole thing to be a great big party and because, with the people they'd invited, there was little chance of it being anything else, formality didn't get a look-in.

It was a sit-down meal, but that was as far as the formality went. Instead of at a high table, Patrick and Annie sat alone at a small table, facing them all, and every one else was grouped around a few circular tables, which made it more relaxed. Not that there would ever have been a problem with that. They all knew each other too well, and trying to keep them in order would have been impossible.

It was beautiful, though. The table settings were simple but smothered in Annie's little touches—more rosebuds, little gifts by each place—the food was superb, the conversation lively and the wine was flowing freely. In short, it was a great party, and Sally's duties for now were over.

She was tempted to dive into her glass head first, but common sense prevailed. She was having enough trouble hanging onto her composure as it was, with Jack so close. The last thing she needed was to lose her fragile grip on her inhibitions! If she'd only known who 'Oz' was, she would have had a serious look at the seating plan, but of course she hadn't known.

And she should have. She really should, because then she could have—what? Not come to her best friend's wedding? Hardly. But she might at least have been prepared for this—and she could have put him somewhere else. There was nowhere that would have been far enough away, but even the other side of Fliss and Tom would have been better.

As it was, David was on her left, with Meg Maguire, now unmistakably pregnant, next to him, and then her husband Ben next to Fliss and Tom Whittaker, and then Jack. On her right. Next to her, so close she could feel him breathe.

He had been born to wear black tie, the stark white shirt contrasting sharply with his golden skin, the cut of the jacket showing off the breadth of his shoulders and the neat, narrow waist. Thank God he was sitting down and she didn't have to look at the cut of his trousers. Every time she looked at him, her heart crashed against her ribs. She was so achingly aware of him it was a miracle she didn't have a neon sign on her head. She probably didn't need one. Her cheeks were probably doing that job all on their own.

And because the table was circular and there were seven of them squeezed up together, their knees kept brushing.

By accident? She wasn't sure, but she kept her legs

clamped firmly together and out of the way, and every little touch sent wildfire racing through her veins.

And then it was time for the speeches, and they all shuffled back from the table and turned so they could see better, and as his knees moved away from hers, she felt the tension go out of her as if her strings had been cut.

Lord, he was nervous.

Nervous, and more aware of Sally than he'd ever been of anyone in his life. Except her, of course. He'd always been utterly aware of her, and that sleeveless, strapless bodice topped by the soft swell of her breasts—hell, he was going to choke in a minute.

Jack ran his finger round the suddenly tight collar of his shirt and wondered how long it would be before he could shed the dratted tie and release its stranglehold on his neck. Stop thinking about her. Listen to the others, he told himself, and watching Annie's father's notes rattle in his hand, and the emotion pucker his features, he forgot about Sally and his nerves and reminded himself what he was doing there.

To see Patrick, his closest and probably only true friend, take the plunge and get married again. He was amazed he'd had the guts to do it after the last time. Ellie had been twenty-three, bright and bubbly and wonderful, and three days after the wedding she'd had a massive stroke. It had nearly killed her, and at the time he'd thought it would kill Patrick, but he'd found the strength to stick by her for the next nine incredibly long years as she'd lain unmoving in a coma, and last year she'd slipped quietly away with Patrick at her side, faithful to the last. Not many men would have shown such unswerving loyalty and faithfulness, but he'd promised to love her in sickness and in health, and he'd done it, for nearly a decade. Was he thinking about Ellie now, perhaps haunted by that earlier tragedy?

He flicked a glance at him. No. He was looking at Annie as if he couldn't believe his luck. Just as he should. Ellie was his past. Annie was his future, and if Jack hadn't loved him like a brother, he would almost have envied him. Annie was beautiful, her love for her new husband shining in her eyes, and even an old cynic like him could see it was a match made in heaven.

Her father evidently thought so, too. His speech was a touching welcome to Patrick, 'the first man I've ever met who I thought was good enough for my daughter', which brought a lump to Jack's throat, and when they all lifted their glasses to toast the bride and groom, he couldn't speak.

Patrick's reply was simple, short and nearly finished the job Annie's father had started. For all his cynicism, Jack found himself swallowing hard as Patrick spoke.

'I have to thank you, Ed, not only for your welcome but for your beautiful and loving daughter. You all know that this is a second chance for both of us,' he said quietly. 'I don't want to dwell on the past, today is about the future, a future I didn't even dare to dream of having, and Annie's given me that.' He took her hand and smiled down at her with a tenderness that made Jack's chest ache. 'So I want to take this opportunity to thank her for loving me, for agreeing to become my wife. I want to thank Katie, her daughter, for welcoming me into their family. Thank you, sweetheart,' he said directly to the little girl, and she blushed and smiled back at him, legs swinging. 'And I want to thank all those of you who've supported us both in the past years and months. We wouldn't be here without you, and it's a pleasure and a privilege to share this day with you. Thank you all for coming, and for making such a wonderful day possible.'

There was a moment of silence, then everybody collected themselves and cheered and clapped, and once they'd subsided he cleared his throat and grinned. 'Now, about these beautiful bridesmaids,' he said, and Katie wriggled in her chair, delighted at the attention, her eyes sparkling and her cheeks pink. Jack flicked a quick glance at Sally. Her cheeks were pink, too, but her eyes were downcast and her smile was wry. Beautiful? Oh, yes. Maybe not in the conventional sense, but he'd seen her like no one else had, with her eyes wild with passion, her lips parted, her shyness forgotten…

'Ladies and gentlemen, the bridesmaids!'

Jack dragged his mind back into line and sucked in a deep breath. It was his turn, and if he was really lucky he wouldn't make a complete idiot of himself. He got to his feet, glanced at his notes and chucked them onto the table. They were no good to him. This was his friend. Probably the only true friend he had in the world.

He knew what to say.

Typical, Sally thought. He always had winged it, and he was doing it now, grinning easily as he defused the tension and charmed everyone with that gorgeous, slightly gruff voice and dry delivery.

And, of course, being Jack, he had them all in stitches. He told stories of their wild youth, crazy stories from their backpacking days, none of which were familiar to Sally. How odd, that they hadn't talked at all about a person who'd been so close to him, but, then, they hadn't talked much at all, all those years ago. They'd had other things on their minds, and college pranks had been right down the list...

She made herself concentrate, laughing as he teased Patrick about the fact that he'd already refitted the kitchen for Annie, but also remembering how close they'd come to splitting up because he'd done it as a surprise, and it had backfired. Annie's husband had kept his gambling addiction secret from her for years, and she'd hated the idea that Patrick had hidden anything from her. Did Jack know that? Probably not, but all the people at their table did, because they'd been involved in the planning and execution of the surprise, and for a while they'd all been on tenterhooks, but then Annie had calmed down, Katie had stopped panicking about her selling the house and Patrick had given them back their security.

And his unconditional love.

And if she thought about that for another minute, she was going to cry.

There was another ripple of laughter, and Jack let it die then carried on. 'I'm supposed to be thanking you for your charming toast to our beautiful bridesmaids, but since one's your new stepdaughter and the other your wife's closest friend, they probably wrote that bit for you. If so, they only told the truth, because they are gorgeous, aren't they?' His eyes stroked Sally and she felt her skin tingle and start to colour again. 'Beautiful and charming,' he went on, 'and if it wasn't for the fact that Katie's only eight and Sally's already married, my heart would be in serious trouble. And maybe it is anyway, but I'm still going to claim a dance with both of them once the band strikes up. So drink up, ladies and gentlemen, boys and girls, and get your dancing shoes on, because the band will be ready for you in about half an hour and I...'

He turned to Sally with that lazy, sexy smile, and her chest tightened in panic. What on earth—?

He took her hand.

Took it, and with his eyes never leaving hers feathered a kiss over her knuckles that made her all but whimper.

'I will be waiting.' Then he straightened and said to David with a smile, 'With your permission?'

David gave a short grunt of laughter and served her up to him on a plate. 'Feel free. I hate dancing. You might need to ask her, but as far as I'm concerned you're welcome.'

And Sally could have killed them both.

Finally!

He took the tie off, shrugged off his jacket, loosened his cufflinks and turned back his cuffs. Better. Now all he needed was the strength to ask Sally to dance without losing his dignity completely.

The kids were getting a little wild, and he found his eyes drawn to them.

To Sally's boys, especially.

They were lovely children. The skin under Alex's left eye was tinged with purple in the corner, and his nose was a little puffy, but it didn't seem to have made any difference to his enjoyment of the evening. He was loud and boisterous and cheerful, and his little brother was bubbly and full of fun, just as he remembered Sally.

He flicked a glance at her.

She was talking to Fliss Whittaker, laughing about something one of the children had said, and he felt his throat contract. If it hadn't been for Clare, he might have been with her. They could have been his children, his boys, instead of which he'd gone off and done his duty and she'd met and married David, apparently almost as soon as his back was turned.

'So, what brings you to England apart from the wedding? Patrick tells me you're here for a while.'

Jack turned to Tom, dragging his attention from Sally, and dredged up a grin. 'Oh, a mixture of duty and nostalgia, really. I've been away for years and, rather than just fly in for the wedding and then out again, I thought it would good to touch base again.'

'Base?' Tom said, his brow creasing. 'I thought— Patrick calls you Oz. I just assumed you were Australian.'

'Sort of—I've got dual nationality,' he explained. 'I was born in Australia, but I'm a Brit really. We moved back here years ago when I was twelve but I haven't been back for nearly ten years now.' Apart from a flying visit last year for Ellie's funeral, but now wasn't the time to go into unnecessary details. 'Anyway, my parents are getting older, and the other side of the world is quite a way, so I thought I could revisit a few old haunts, catch up with the old folks, do a bit of hill walking in the Lake District maybe.'

Tom tipped his head on one side thoughtfully. 'So, technically, you might be free at the moment?'

Jack felt his eyes narrow a fraction. 'Free?' he said warily.

Tom grinned ruefully. 'I'm in a jam. One of our registrars has damaged himself playing rugby. Actually it's Patrick's fault, he dragged him into the team and now he's out of action with a broken hand—our second casualty to rugby this season. Patrick mentioned you were going to be around for the next two or three weeks, and I just wondered if you fancied doing a little locum work to tide us over?

Getting adequate cover's a nightmare, and Matt Jordan, one of the other consultants, is in Canada at the moment, so we're really stuffed, and Fliss is going to divorce me if I don't spend a little time at home soon. I don't know if you've kept your registration up to date…'

'Yes,' he said, without giving himself time to analyse it. 'And yes.'

Tom frowned. 'To what?'

'Yes, I have, and, yes, I will. Do the locum. Just for three weeks.'

And God help him, with Sally in the same hospital, but the way he felt, and the way she'd looked at him, he just couldn't walk away.

Was he ever going to ask her to dance?

And did she want him to?

Oh, yes. Any other response would be an outright lie. The music was unashamedly romantic, and the low, heavy beat was making her body ache…

'I'm going to take the boys upstairs and calm them down and get them to bed,' David murmured in her ear. 'They're getting over the top and they're still shattered after the flight yesterday.'

'Thanks,' she said gratefully. Her feet were killing her. She could stand for hours in flat work shoes, but put her in high heels and she was crippled in minutes, especially after flying. And since Jack was networking his way around the room and chatting to all and sundry, she kicked off her shoes under the table and sighed with relief.

Bliss. All she needed now was a huge glass of iced water and she could drink some of it and dribble the rest on her poor, aching toes—

'Dance with me.'

It wasn't an order. Not exactly. More a suggestion. She looked up, struggling to control the racing of her heart, and found Jack staring solemnly down at her.

As if connected to him by some invisible cord, she got to her feet and moved towards him. 'I've taken off my shoes,' she said inanely, stating the obvious.

'Good for you. I'll try not to tread on your toes.'

He held out his hand, and she put hers in it, feeling the warmth as his fingers closed around her own. He led her onto the little dance floor just as the tempo changed and a haunting love song started to play.

He met her eyes, and with a soft sigh he drew her into his arms, rested his forehead against hers and linked his hands behind her back, easing her closer. Their legs meshed, their bodies touched and she felt a huge, forgotten ache invade her chest.

His mouth was right in front of her eyes, his lips soft and full and sensual, slightly parted. She could feel the warmth of his breath against her face, the beat of his heart against her own, the hard, toned muscles of his thighs cradling hers.

And she wanted him. Wanted him in a way she'd forgotten, a way she thought she'd left behind years ago.

One touch had been all it had taken, and the years of her marriage had been wiped out as if they'd never existed. It was as if David had never touched her, never held her, never made a baby with her. She couldn't imagine going to bed with him tonight.

But Jack—oh, yes, her body sighed, softening towards his. She could imagine that, him reaching for her, touching her, her body opening to his...

His mouth moved, his lips pressing together, his jaw working as he swallowed. She could feel the change in his body, the shift, the pressure as he unlinked his hands and slid them flat over her back, one cradling her shoulders, the other sliding down to cup her bottom, easing her even closer. His solid, hard thigh wedged between hers, bringing them into intimate alignment and leaving nothing to her imagination.

Her breath caught, and she turned her head, resting it on his shoulder, her face turned towards his neck in case anybody should read the expression on her face. She ought to move away, to make some space between them, but it was beyond her.

She felt the brush of his lips against her temple, and her breath sucked in and out in a tiny sob of frustration and confusion. Why had he come back? She'd been happy with David. They had a good marriage.

Didn't they?

And if so, why was she feeling like this, as if it had never existed, gone in an instant, as fleeting as a dream? One of those strange, confusing dreams where nothing really made sense, where you went through a door and up some stairs and came out in a different house, or into a street, or couldn't find your way home.

Except she had.

Here, now, in Jack's arms she felt as if she'd finally found her way home.

CHAPTER THREE

How could it be?

Nine, nearly ten years, wiped away in an instant. Just the touch of her hair against his cheek, the feel of her body, soft and warm and tender against his own, and all the forgotten moments had come flooding back, the passion, the laughter, the intimate little moments that they'd shared all too briefly.

The party was over now. He'd slipped away into the darkness and found a deserted bench in the garden, snagging a half-empty wine bottle off a table on the way past. Stupid, to imagine that drinking it would take away the feel of her body against his, drown out the clamouring of his blood. Still, he tipped it up to his lips, filling his mouth with the unwanted and unnecessary alcohol in a vain attempt to numb his raging body.

What the hell was he doing? He ought to go. If he hadn't already had too much to drink he would have got into his car and gone back to Patrick and Annie's house and packed his things.

Except he'd made a commitment to dog-sit for them while they were away on their honeymoon—no, not honeymoon, Patrick didn't want it called that—and he'd made a commitment to cover for Tom Whittaker's registrar for the next three weeks.

Damn.

Oh, well. He tipped the bottle again. If he couldn't escape, he might as well make it as painless as possible.

'Drowning your sorrows, Oz?'

He scowled up at Patrick in the dark. 'Haven't you got anything better to do on your wedding night than creep up on me?'

Patrick laughed softly and Jack felt the bench beside him give a little. 'Not at the moment. Annie's putting Katie to bed, and, anyway, I wanted to talk to you. I've hardly had a chance today.'

His internal radar started to bleep a warning. 'No, it's been a bit busy. Great day, though,' he said, trying to head him off, but Patrick wasn't having any of it.

'Yes, it was. Fantastic. I'm glad you could make it, but I'm not sure about Sally.'

He went still. 'Sally?' he said cautiously.

'Oh, come on, Oz. We go way back. I know you inside out. What's the story?' Patrick's voice was soft, coaxing in the darkness, and he sighed and surrendered to the inevitable. It was time he told him.

'We had an affair—probably the briefest and hottest on record.'

'And?'

'And Clare turned up and told me she was pregnant. Said if I wanted to see my child, I'd marry her.'

'But—'

'I know. Now. But not then. So I left Sal, and I married Clare. And I made what was probably the biggest mistake of my life.'

There was a long silence, then Patrick exhaled sharply. 'Hell, I'm sorry. I had no idea, you didn't tell me.'

'You were up to your eyes with Ellie. It was only a few months after her stroke. I wasn't going to come and bleat to you about the mess my love life was in, was I? But, God, I needed to. I could have done with a shoulder at that time.'

'And I didn't even realise.' Patrick's breath eased out on a sigh. 'I'm so sorry I wasn't there for you.' He was quiet for a moment, then he said in a low voice, 'Oz, don't mess with Sally. Things aren't really good between her and David. Annie doesn't know why, and Sally hasn't said anything, but she doesn't look happy.'

He sighed. 'I noticed—but don't worry. I won't upset the apple cart. Three weeks and I'm out of here. And even I can keep my hands to myself for three weeks.'

'It's not your hands I'm worried about,' Patrick said softly. 'It's your heart—and hers.' He felt a hand rest briefly on Jack's shoulder, then there was a crunch of gravel and the bench shifted. 'Take care, my friend. Of both of you.'

He grunted. 'Never mind about me. Go and make love to your beautiful wife before she falls asleep.'

'Oh, I intend to,' Patrick said softly, and Jack stifled a pang of regret. He'd made his bed with Clare nine years ago. And David was in Sally's. Were they making love right now?

Hell.

No. He wouldn't think about it. He'd just get through the night, and then he'd be free—except he'd promised to work in the same damned hospital as her.

Well, he'd just have to keep his head down and avoid her. Hospitals were big places. It couldn't be that hard.

* * *

'Have you missed me?'

Angie laughed wryly and threw Sally a grin. 'I haven't had time to notice! You're on Triage this morning, to ease you back in. Don't want to shock you too much. How was the wedding?'

'Fabulous,' she said truthfully. 'I haven't had so much fun in ages. It was a really fantastic party, and coming right after our holiday like that was perfect. I feel really refreshed.'

'Good. I'm really glad you enjoyed it. You were looking tired.'

'I was. The break's done us good.' Not that David had said much since the wedding, but that was par for the course.

'I gather Tom's stolen one of the wedding guests to locum for us.'

She frowned. 'Really? Who?'

'Jack Logan. He's going to cover for Al.'

No! Sally felt her colour drain, then flood back. 'Ah— sorry, I feel a bit queasy. I need some air—must be the jet-lag still. Give me a minute and I'll go and get set up in the triage room.'

And she escaped, heart pounding, legs like jelly.

Not Jack. Not here, in her department, right underfoot where she couldn't get him out of her mind. She was having enough trouble as it was.

She hadn't seen him again after that dance. She'd excused herself and gone to check on the boys, and she hadn't come down again. Cowardly? Perhaps, or perhaps just prudent. Whatever, he'd left the next day, Wednesday—heavens, was that only yesterday?—before they'd come down for breakfast, and she'd felt a pang of regret mixed with the relief, and quickly crushed it.

And today she'd rushed around, sorting out the kids

and ferrying them to holiday club before coming to work, and now, just when she'd hoped she'd be so busy she didn't have time to think about him, he was going to be here for days!

Weeks?

Her legs threatened to crumple again. Please, God, not weeks.

She took a steadying breath and went back inside, picking up the first set of notes. 'Mrs Collier?'

'Hiding from me?'

The soft, gruff words had her head snapping up. She shot him a mocking smile and sucked in some air. 'Hardly. Why would I?'

'I have no idea, but we've got a big RTA coming in and Tom wants us to work together. He says you'll keep me out of mischief.'

She'd keep them both out of mischief, she thought, given enough strength to do so. 'So who's on Triage if I leave it?'

He shrugged, those broad, strong shoulders shifting under his shirt. 'That's not my worry. You are.'

'Oh, you don't need to worry about me, Jack,' she told him firmly. 'I know exactly what I'm doing.'

Running, as hard as she could, in the opposite direction!

She was great to work with.

As she'd said, she knew exactly what she was doing, and she seemed to know what he was doing, too, so although he'd never been there before or worked with her in this way, he found her anticipating his needs, handing him things, doing others without having to be asked, and once their patient was stable and away to Theatre she cleared the area, checked the stock and sorted it out herself.

'Why don't you delegate that to a junior member of staff?' he asked, and she blinked at him in surprise.

'Because I know what we've used, I know your preferences now, and I've made sure we're equipped for that as well as for anyone else who might be in here. And nobody else could do it as fast or as easily, so it makes sense.'

It did, and it also made sense that she worried about that sort of thing. She'd never been one for letting things happen by chance. Even the first time they'd made love, she'd been in control of when and where, and had set the scene. Beautifully.

And he really didn't need to think about that when he was dressed in flimsy scrubs and the department was crawling with onlookers!

'Right, I'm going back to Triage now,' she said firmly, as their patients were all sorted and the place had quietened down. He watched her go with a mixture of relief and regret and, letting out a sharp sigh, he went to find Tom and volunteer his services for the next case.

'We need to talk.'

She looked up from the ironing and frowned at the serious tone of David's voice. 'What about?'

'Us,' he said, and with a sudden disquieting sense of inevitability, she turned off the iron, put it down on the heatproof rest and met his eyes.

'Us?'

He nodded. She could see a pulse beating in his neck, and his mouth was set in a grim line. 'Come and sit down. This isn't easy and I don't really know where to start.'

She went, her legs suddenly weak and her heart pounding, and sat beside him on the sofa. He took her hand, resting it on his lap and staring down at it as if he was looking for the words there on her skin.

She couldn't help him. She was filled with the guilt of her disloyalty, of her feelings for Jack so recently reawakened and never, it seemed, really gone. So she waited, and after an age he said abruptly, as if it was the only way he could get the words out, 'I can't do this any more. I can't live a lie. Being with you, pretending everything's fine, finding excuses for not making love to you…'

He broke off and she stared at their joined hands, puzzled by his words. OK, so they hadn't made love since the wedding but they hadn't made love before the wedding, either—not for ages. Months. Not this year, certainly, and it was already April. And not for ages before that. He hadn't suggested it and, to be honest, neither had she. So that wasn't new, and it couldn't be anything to do with Jack, so what, then?

'Why is it a lie?'

He shrugged, his brow furrowed as if he was struggling for the right words. 'Seeing Annie and Patrick together at the wedding, realising what it ought to be like—it isn't like that for us, and it never has been, but that's what it should be like. *Could* be like.' He took a deep breath, then said hurriedly, 'Sally, I'm in love.'

In love? David was in love?

And then it hit her. All the hours he'd worked late, all the times he'd phoned and said he'd be another hour, all the times he'd worked at the weekend. She'd even joked about it, said if she didn't know better she'd think he was having an affair with his PA…

'It's Wendy, isn't it?' she asked, her voice not quite steady, and he nodded.

'Yes, it's Wendy—and I love her, as I never thought I could ever love again.'

And something in the tone of his voice as he spoke Wendy's name made her realise it was the truth. He'd never said *her* name like that, like a caress. Oh, dear God. She tried to pull her hand away, but he held on, tightening his grip, his face working.

'We haven't done anything,' he said gruffly. 'We aren't having an affair. It wasn't right—not while I'm still here with you and the boys.'

'But you want to.'

He nodded. 'Yes, we want to. I want to marry her, Sally. I want to have the right to look at her as Patrick looked at Annie. I want to have children with her—go to bed with her, wake up with her, for the rest of my life. But I didn't want to hurt you. You've been hurt enough—and then I saw you with Jack, dancing, and it all suddenly made perfect sense. It's him, isn't it? He's the one.'

Oh, lord. He knew. Her heart thudded, but there was no point in denying it, so she nodded, and she felt his hand tighten on hers, squeezing it comfortingly.

'Funny, how you've never mentioned his name, but it didn't seem important. If I'd known, maybe I could have helped you at the wedding, but I was missing Wendy and wondering how to tell you, and I wasn't a lot of use to you, was I?'

She found a smile from somewhere. 'You didn't have to give me to him quite so enthusiastically when he asked if he could dance with me,' she chided gently, and he groaned and rubbed a hand over his face.

'Sorry. God, you must have wanted to kill me, but I just didn't think—I didn't realise until later, when I saw you dancing. Is it going to make everything very complicated?'

She gave a little huff of despairing laughter. 'I hope not. He's only here three weeks.'

'Nevertheless—you've never got over him, have you? I thought I hadn't got over Jess, never would, but when I met Wendy I realised I could love again—really love, like Patrick and Annie. And going on as we are, it's just—I can't do it any longer. Life's not a dress rehearsal. Heard that so many times, but it's true. And I don't want to throw this chance of happiness away. If I felt you were happy with me—'

'What? You'd throw away your chance with Wendy? No. I can't let you do that. I *am* happy, though,' Sally added. 'You've given me so much. And if I'm not, it's not your fault. You've been the best friend—'

'But not your soul-mate.'

She swallowed, trying not to think of Jack. 'No. Not my soul-mate,' she agreed. 'And if you feel that much for Wendy, then of course you should be together.'

He nodded, then his fingers tightened on hers. 'It's just the boys…'

He broke off, and a tear slid down his cheek and splashed on their hands. 'It's going to really cut them up. I'm so sorry.'

She pulled her hand free, put her arm round his shoulders and pulled him into her arms. 'Don't be,' she said softly. 'You've been a wonderful father to the boys, and I can never regret that, and we've been good friends, but really that's all, you're right, and if you can have what Patrick and Annie have got, then you should…'

Her voice cracked, and he wrapped her in his arms and rocked her against his chest while they both wept for the loss of their marriage, the failure, the regrets, the guilt—so many feelings, but there was no surprise.

She'd known it was coming. It had been coming for years, but Wendy starting work for him nine months ago had been the catalyst for this. That and the wedding. And Jack.

She straightened up and sniffed, groping in her pocket for a tissue and scrubbing at her nose.

'So when are you moving out?' she asked, struggling for control of an uncontrollable situation.

'I don't know. I need to talk to Wendy and the boys.'

'Will you go to her house?'

'I don't know. It depends what you think, what the boys think, but I can't stay here any more. Not now. Not now I've made the decision and talked to you.'

'No.' No, he couldn't stay, she could see that, even though it would seem so strange without him. Then the enormity of it struck her, and she shook her head, staring at him in dismay. 'How are we going to tell the boys?'

'Together. We'll do it tomorrow. Not tonight, there's no point. They might as well sleep, and give us time to come to terms with it. Come on, you need to go to bed.'

Bed? Bed? she thought hysterically. Which bed?

But David just smiled a sad smile. 'It's OK. I need to see Wendy—and then I'll come back and sleep on the sofa.'

'You will come back—before the morning? I can't tell the boys on my own.'

'I'll come back. I promise.'

She knew he would. David didn't break his promises.

Well, not until now.

She listened to the front door close, his car pull out of the drive, and then she went upstairs, to the room she'd shared with her husband, and got into the bed she'd slept in with him last night, and wondered how on earth they'd tell the boys.

'You look like hell.'

She stared into Jack's sombre face blankly, and it started to blur. 'I'm sorry—I can't—'

His fingers caught her chin, turning her back towards him. 'Sal, what's happened?' he said, his voice gentle.

Damn. She'd thought she could do this, thought she could cope, but apparently not. She shook her head, all her emotions suddenly rushing to the surface and threatening to swamp her. 'David…'

'Is he ill?'

She shook her head again. 'No. He's…' She couldn't finish, couldn't bring herself to say 'left me'. 'There's someone else,' she said eventually, and he swore under his breath and threw his arm round her shoulders, guiding her out of the department, down a corridor and into an empty room.

She didn't know whose. She didn't care. It didn't matter. Nothing mattered any more.

He shut the door, propped himself against it, arms folded, and fixed her with those all-seeing slate-blue eyes. 'Tell me,' he said softly.

'He's in love with his PA—Wendy,' she said, still wondering over the way he'd said the word. Funny, when she said it, it was just a name, but on David's lips…

'Does he know you know?'

She nodded. 'Oh, yes. He told me on Friday. We told the boys on Saturday morning, then yesterday afternoon he took them to meet her and her daughter, and see the house, and then he brought them back and went—moved out. Well, some of his things, anyway. He's got the rest to move some time, I suppose.'

And the children would have to endure it, watching him carrying his possessions out of the house, breaking up their home…

'What brought it on?'

'I think it's been coming for ages, but it was the wedding that did it.'

'Because of me?'

She shook her head. 'Not really,' she said, and it was true. Maybe it had just been the catalyst. Her eyes filled again and she scrubbed them angrily. 'Because of Annie and Patrick being so happy. It just brought his feelings to the surface, made him realise what he was missing.' She gave a tiny, humourless laugh. 'So much for me telling you I didn't have a loveless marriage, but I really didn't think it was.'

He made a soft sound of commiseration. 'And now?'

'Now I can't believe I was so stupid. And I can't think about it now, I have to work. I can't let this get in the way.'

'But people need to know. Tom, Angie—they're not just friends, they're colleagues, and they need to know so they can watch out for you.'

'I don't want them watching out for me,' she protested, but he just raised a brow.

'I think you have a professional duty to tell them that you may not be up to scratch.'

'I am up to scratch.'

'I don't think so. Your husband's just moved out, your marriage is over—even if he wasn't the love of your life, you've still got the upset of the kids. Of course you aren't going to be functioning right. Where are the kids, by the way?'

'With David,' she said tonelessly. 'At the office. They were supposed to be going to holiday club but we didn't think it would be a good idea today. He came over at six-thirty just before I left.'

'So there's nobody at home? You could go back and rest?'

She felt panic rising in her chest. 'Jack, don't make me go home. I can't stand it there, it's so empty.'

'Ah, hell,' he muttered, and shrugging away from the door he dragged her into his arms, crushing her against his chest and mumbling furiously against her hair. She couldn't understand him, couldn't hear the words, but she didn't think they were complimentary. 'Stay here,' he said, releasing her at last. 'I'll go and tell them we're taking a break, and we're going out for coffee. Then you can come back and Angie can find you something to do.'

'Triage,' she suggested, but he shook his head.

'No. Not Triage. Cubicles. And I'll work with you. Sit. Stay,' he said, and she wondered a little hysterically if she was expected to wag her tail.

Damn.

How could David have done that? Broken up their marriage, torn the kids' lives apart? It was just as well he wasn't there, or he would have been torn apart—literally. Jack's hands were itching.

He slapped the door out of the way and stalked into the central corridor just as Tom Whittaker came out of Resus. He frowned at Jack.

'What flew up your skirt?'

'David's left Sally,' he said in a terse undertone.

Tom's face was shocked. 'What? When? They were fine at the wedding—well, as fine as they've been for a few months.'

'Exactly. I'm taking her out for a bit. She won't go home, so I'll take her back to the Corrigans' and feed her and give her coffee, and then I want Angie to find her something busy and harmless to do.'

'I'll sort that out. I take it she wants this under wraps?'

He nodded. 'I think so.'

Tom tilted his head on one side. 'Do you two have—um…?'

'History? Yes,' he replied shortly. 'And, no, the break-up was nothing to do with me. I don't trash marriages.'

Tom nodded, clearly satisfied with his reply. 'Take care of her. She's special.'

'I know.'

He took her back to Annie's. Her legs were moving automatically, and once inside he pushed her gently down onto the sofa. Scruff, the elderly and affectionate lurcher the Corrigans had rescued from a homeless and equally elderly patient, climbed up beside her and snuggled into her side, and she fondled his ears and tried not to cry.

'You're not supposed to be on the new sofa,' she told him, but he just thumped his tail and licked her.

'I'll get coffee,' Jack said, and he disappeared into the kitchen and came back after a few minutes with a tray of goodies. Coffee, toast, marmalade, biscuits—lots of different sorts—and set the tray down in front of her.

She looked at it, at the array of biscuits, and started to laugh. 'Are you feeding me up?' she said, struggling for common sense, and he sat down on the other side of the dog and poured the coffee.

'Absolutely. When did you last eat?'

She shrugged. 'Can't remember.'

'Start with toast,' he advised, and smeared a slice with lashings of butter and marmalade and shoved it into her hand. 'Eat.'

So she ate. She ate two slices, and one of the stem ginger oat cookies, and she drank two mugs of coffee, and gradually the cold, numb feeling started to fade. She put her mug down and smiled at him tiredly. 'Thanks,' she murmured. 'I needed that.'

'My pleasure. I have to go back. Why don't you stay here with the dog and have a sleep?'

'I have to work,' she protested, but he shook his head.

'No, you don't. Not today. Take today to think, to sleep, to sort your head out a little. The world won't come to a halt because you aren't running on the treadmill for a few hours, you know,' he told her with a gentle, teasing smile, and she tried to smile back and failed. And, anyway, the thought was so tempting…

'OK,' she said reluctantly. 'I'll take an hour or so.'

She took five, curled asleep on her side, the dog snuggled against her tummy like a great shaggy teddy bear, and that was how Jack found her when he came back at four to check on her.

Sally pushed her hair out of her eyes and tried to sit up. Scruff licked her chin, ambled off the sofa and stretched, and then wagged his scraggly old tail at Jack.

'You been looking after her, boy?' he said softly, and the tail waved again. He sat down where the dog had been, one hand on the back of the sofa, the other lifting a strand of hair she'd missed away from her face. He hadn't meant to touch her, but somehow there seemed no place for distance now.

'Sleep well?'

She sank back against the cushion and nodded, staring up at him blurrily. 'What time is it?' she murmured.

'Four.'

Her eyes flew open wider, and she struggled into a sitting position, hooking her legs up under her and staring at him in consternation. 'It can't be four! David's got a meeting—I have to fetch the boys!'

'What time?'

'Four-thirty—I wasn't going to have the day off!'

'Well, you clearly needed it,' he said matter-of-factly. 'It'll get better. Give it a few more days and you'll get everything in perspective.'

She made a rude noise and pushed him out of the way, getting to her feet and then swaying. 'Oh—head rush,' she mumbled, and he caught her against his chest and steadied her, relishing her softness and wishing he had the right to hold her like this all the time, but he didn't. She stood there for a few seconds, then straightened up and stepped back, avoiding his eyes. Good thing, too. God knows what she would have seen.

'I have to go.'

'I'll give you a lift. Where's your car?'

'In the car park on the other side of the hospital.'

'Come on, then.'

He'd lied.

A few more days didn't give her any perspective. It gave her a huge pain inside where the numbness had been, an aching void that threatened to fill with failure and misery, and she didn't know how she'd cope at the weekend, when the boys went to stay with David and Wendy.

What those days did, though, was help her realise that it was nothing to do with David. She didn't miss him—he'd been such a small part of her life for so long now that she hardly noticed the difference, and the idea of jealousy didn't even cross her mind. Wendy was welcome to him—she was even glad for them. It was the boys she was worried about, and the boys she missed when they were with David.

It was the little things that were beginning to dawn on her—things like birthdays and Christmases and school plays—how would they decide which parent was involved, or would it all be frightfully civilised?

It was too much to take in and deal with, so she'd tried to lose herself in work, starting the next day, unwilling to take any time off, and her colleagues had said nothing but had let her know in all sorts of little ways how much they cared.

And it drove her crazy.

She wanted to get on with it, to ignore her home life and pretend it didn't exist, but she couldn't because the boys needed her. It was the school holidays, of course, and under normal circumstances they'd be at holiday club, but the circumstances were far from normal, so she engineered her rota and freed up Thursday and Friday so she could spend them with the boys, volunteering for the night shift on Friday evening and the day shift on Sunday. Anything rather than sit alone in the house until the boys came back on Sunday night.

And then she found out Jack was working late on

Friday, after she'd already said she'd do the shift, and she wondered whose side God was on, because it certainly wasn't hers. The last thing she needed was to be working with him throughout a long night when she was already emotionally exhausted.

Still, it was only till ten or so, midnight at the latest. Then someone else would take over, and she'd be able to relax.

CHAPTER FOUR

THEY ended up working together in Resus.

Side by side. Hip to hip. Hand to hand.

Their patient was a young man who'd been on his way from a pub to a club when he'd been jumped on and kicked repeatedly by a gang of youths.

'He's got a flail chest,' Sally said, cutting away his clothes, and Jack swivelled his eyes to watch the broken section of ribcage collapsing in when his chest lifted, and bulging out when it fell.

'Damn. Get him on 100 per cent oxygen and try and wedge something against it to stop it. He's having enough problems without that.'

'Neurological?'

Jack's eyes flicked back to his patient's face. 'I think his right pupil's slightly larger. Any second now it's going to flare—oh, hell. Why am I always right? It's gone.'

'Just the one?'

He nodded shortly. 'Damn. Somebody book him an urgent CT scan, please! I reckon he's got a nasty bleed or his brain's swelling so fast it's herniating. And we'd better book chest as well while we're at it, because he's mashed this side of his ribs and he's got to be bleeding in there.

Sal, I'm going to intubate him. I don't want him getting cerebral anoxia and if we hyperventilate it'll lower the arterial PCO2 and might help minimise his cerebral oedema. And I want a full set of head, chest and spinal films while we wait for the scan.'

They worked furiously, putting him on CPAP so that the pressure would keep his oxygen saturation high to try and minimise the damage, and as soon as a slot was free he was wheeled down to the scanner, a chest drain in place. The neurologist was working with them by this time, and at a little after two the patient went to Theatre to have a huge clot removed from his brain.

What happened next would be in the lap of the gods, but they'd done all they could. On autopilot, Sally sorted out Resus, fell into a chair in the staffroom and closed her eyes, exhausted. She didn't know where Jack had gone—home, probably, since he had only been covering the evening, she thought—but then she heard footsteps, and someone fiddling with mugs, and the chair beside her creaked.

'Tea?'

She cracked an eye open, took the mug from him and sighed with relief.

'Thanks. Couldn't be bothered to make it.'

'I know the feeling. What are you doing here tonight, by the way?'

She shut the eye again. 'Working.'

'Or avoiding the house?'

She opened both eyes and fixed him with a look. 'I have to learn to cope with it, I know, but just for now I'm happier here. And in any case, I spent yesterday and today with the boys.'

'You could always have the night off. I can't believe you're that strapped for cash.'

She glared at him. 'That's nothing to do with it. I can't just dump my commitment to the department. It's bad enough juggling shifts—and anyway, when I work is none of your business. Don't nag me, Jack.'

'I wouldn't dream of it. I seem to remember doing the same thing myself in the past—working myself to a stand-still, trying to forget.'

Forget what? He didn't say, and she couldn't ask, because she couldn't speak. Ben's face swam in front of her, hurt and confused and uncertain, and she couldn't deal with it. She shut her eyes again and turned her attention back to her tea. She didn't need to see to drink, and if her eyes were shut there was just the vaguest chance of her keeping the tears firmly trapped where they belonged.

'Ah, Sal,' he said softly, taking her cup from her hands, and then her head was tucked into the angle of his shoulder, snuggled against his chin, and his big, strong arms were round her, and she could feel his even, steady breathing and the solid beat of his heart comfortingly just beneath her ear.

She felt the tears dribble down her cheeks. 'They're just so confused,' she said miserably. 'They don't understand what went wrong. They hardly know him now. It's been months since they've seen much of him—apart from our holiday, and he was hardly with us then in spirit. Looking back on it, I don't know how I didn't realise! And every night he had to check in with the office and talk on the phone for hours. I must be so naïve.'

'No. You trusted him. You should be able to do that with your partner.'

She thought about that for a moment, then tilted her head and looked up at him. 'Could you trust Clare?'

He gave a bitter little laugh. 'Not as far as I could throw her.'

She straightened up so she could look at him properly, but his face was unreadable. 'Really? Are you sure you aren't judging her by your own standards? Maybe she feels she can't trust you because when she came to tell you she was pregnant she found you with me.'

Naked, but she wasn't saying that bit out loud. She didn't have to. It was a scene she was sure neither of them would forget in a lifetime.

'We'd finished,' he said firmly. 'I wasn't cheating on her, Sal. I wouldn't have done that to either of you. And I had no idea that she was pregnant. Besides which—'

'Oh, great, you're together. We've had a call for a team to go an RTA—there's an entrapment and possible arm amputation and the orthos are all tied up and the rapid response team's already out. How's your field surgery?'

Sally was already on her feet, following Jack out of the door as she scrubbed the tears from her cheeks. She heard him tell Tom, 'Peachy. It's what I do best.'

'Good. Go do it, then. Sally will tell you what to take. Your transport's outside, waiting for you.'

She was already grabbing the bags filled with emergency surgical kit, there was an anaesthetist running down the corridor towards them. They headed for the doors, shoving their arms into hi-vis coats as they went, so there was no more time to talk, no time to ask what he'd been going to say.

'Got any more details?' the anaesthetist asked as they piled into the car.

Jack laughed. 'Not a thing. Hope you know where you're going,' he said to the driver.

'Absolutely. Hang onto your hats.'

The blue lights came on and they streaked out of the hospital grounds and through the outskirts of the town, picking up the busy trunk-road in minutes. The roads were quiet by trunk-road standards, but as they approached the accident they could see flashing blue lights up ahead and everything was at a standstill.

There was a narrow passage through between the cars, and the driver wove through it, siren blipping every few seconds to warn the occupants of the stationary cars. Sometimes people opened their doors to try and get a look and didn't think to check their mirrors, and, judging by the look of it, they'd got enough to do already without collecting casualties along the way.

He pulled up and they were out, dragging the equipment with them and running towards the waving paramedic by one of the vehicles.

'What have you got for us?' Jack asked, taking charge.

'Woman trapped by the arm. The fire crew are doing their best but she's got a tension pneumothorax and maybe a tear in her aorta. Her BP's dropping steadily and her sats are low.' He reeled off the figures and the medication he'd given her, but then added, 'She needs more pain relief. She's complaining more about her chest than her arm, which worries me.'

Jack nodded. 'That fits with the aorta. She needs to be out of there fast. Can we hustle them?'

The man shook his head. 'I have done, they're going flat out, but they can't do it fast enough, it's just not possible.'

And it wasn't just the aorta that was a problem. There

was the danger of crush syndrome if she was left too long and then released, and that could be fatal, too.

'Name?'

'Jennifer. Couldn't catch the surname. We've taken her husband's body out of the car to get access to her. Someone's checking it for ID. He died instantly—we haven't told her.'

Oh, lord. Sally squirmed into the car behind the woman and put a hand on her shoulder, acknowledging the paramedic holding her head still. 'Jennifer, I'm Sally, and that's Jack just coming in beside you. Hang on, my love, we'll get you out as soon as we can.'

She reached up and pulled off her oxygen mask. 'He's dead, isn't he? My husband. I saw him, but nobody will tell me. They keep changing the subject, but I need to know.'

Jack's hand reached out and brushed the hair gently back from her face. 'Yes, he is dead. I'm really sorry. Let's get you out of here and we can talk about it more later. For now just put the mask back on, sweetheart, and let's have a look at you.'

He did a rapid assessment, then told her what Sally had been expecting, that she would have to lose her left arm. It was trapped in the tangled wreckage of the door, crushed beyond recovery, the circulation to it was totally destroyed and there was no way it was coming out in one piece.

And she knew it, too. She reached up her right hand and caught Jack's sleeve as he retreated to let the anaesthetist in. 'Jack? Ask them to find my wedding ring,' she begged, and Sally saw his face tighten just for a second.

'Sure. We'll find it and keep it for you.'

'Thank you. I couldn't bear to lose it…'

Her eyelids drooped, and Sally called after him, 'She's going.'

'OK. Right, let's get this roof off if we can and get in there fast. Sally, can you come and scrub?'

'Sure.' She gave Jennifer's shoulder a quick squeeze as Peter, the anaesthetist, crawled into the front beside their patient and assessed her airway.

'I'll get her under—can you hang on here for a sec while I intubate? I'll need to do a jaw thrust because of the risk of neck injury and I'll need help.'

So she was in there while the fire brigade were cutting through the pillars with the jaws of life, chomping through the metal as if it were nothing and lifting the roof away to give better access while she held the woman's jaw forward for Peter and the paramedic held her head until they could slip a collar on her.

She scrubbed in the back of the ambulance, as well as possible, and gloved and gowned she scrambled back over the seats to help. Jack was already in there beside Peter, carefully shifting Jennifer to get better access to her arm.

'She's crashing,' Peter warned, and Jack shook his head, abandoned finesse and did the quickest amputation Sally had ever seen. Not that she'd seen many, but it was fast and slick and the woman was out, the bleeding vessels were clamped off and she was away in the ambulance, with Jack and Peter working on her.

As the doors closed, Jack yelled, 'Sal, get the ring!'

She turned back to the fireman who had the job of sorting out the chaos. 'Can we get to her hand? I need to take it back to the hospital anyway but she was fretting about her wedding ring.'

'Do our best. Give me a minute, I'll have a look.'

And a minute later he emerged, a slightly bent and bloody gold ring in the palm of his hand. 'This what you wanted? I'm afraid the hand isn't coming out any time soon.'

She took the ring, her eyes suddenly filling. 'Thank you.'

Slipping it carefully into a zipped pocket, she went back to the car and returned to the hospital.

It was four-thirty. The sky was still dark, the air cold and crisp. She shivered as she walked towards the doors, and then Jack was there, slinging an arm around her shoulders and giving her a quick squeeze. 'You OK?'

She nodded wordlessly, her eyes asking a question, and he nodded.

'She's in Theatre. They're patching her aorta and the ortho reg is sorting out her arm. I gather she's stabilised and they're hopeful.'

'Family?'

'They've contacted them. Did you manage to find the ring?'

She unzipped the pocket and pulled it out, holding it out to him on the palm of her hand. They both stared at it, deeply conscious of the symbolism of the battered little band.

Jack lifted it carefully from her hand and slipped it into his pocket. 'I'll take it up to her later. I'll be going up to see her anyway. I checked her husband while they were taking the roof off. It would have been instant and painless. It's not much, but I can give her that. And the ring.'

She nodded.

It was only a matter of days since she'd watched Patrick slide a ring onto Annie's finger with sure, steady hands. Her own was sitting in her jewellery box. She didn't quite know what to do with it, but wearing it didn't seem an option.

Such a tiny thing, a wedding ring, but so full of meaning.

Broken promises, love lost, vows severed by fate.

She turned away, walking quickly down the corridor into the ladies' loo and shutting herself away until the wave of emotion retreated. Then she came out, washed her face and hands, changed into a fresh set of scrubs and went back out into the fray.

The day stretched out endlessly.

Sally went home to bed after her shift finished, couldn't sleep properly and got up again at two, but the house was so empty without the boys that she couldn't stand it, so she had a shower, pulled on her jeans and a jumper and went out in the car.

She didn't know where she was going—for a walk? Shopping? There was no food in the house and the boys would be back tomorrow, so it probably wouldn't be a bad idea, but it held no appeal.

And then she found herself outside Annie's house, hovering in the road and questioning her motives—motives she hadn't even realised she'd had.

What was she doing there? Jack wouldn't want to see her—and even if he did, that was even more dangerous! She was starting to lean on him too much—every time she went to work he was there, his lazy grin and watchful eyes following her round the department, dragging her off for breaks every now and again, keeping her focussed and fed.

Not that she needed to be fed. She'd been comfort-eating all week—chocolate and crisps and rubbish food generally, although she hadn't cooked a single thing for herself that could in any way be called a meal. She'd cooked for the boys, of course, but they hadn't always been there, or sometimes they'd eaten with friends or with David.

Fliss had been brilliant, taking them under her wing and blending them seamlessly with her huge and tumultuous family, and they were getting there. The shock was receding, the fear that they'd lose either of their parents proving unfounded.

And kids were resilient. She knew that. She was the one who was most unsettled by it all, and she wondered how much of it was to do with David leaving her and how much to do with Jack coming back into her life with his laughing eyes and irresistible attraction.

And here she was, outside the house where he was staying—probably sleeping right now. He'd been up all night, like her, and he'd probably had the sense to spend the day in bed.

Oh, lord. Warm and sleep-rumpled, with his hair sticking up like the boys' and his eyes soft with sleep, and wearing nothing but a lazy come-hither smile. He would be naked, of course. He was always naked in bed. She'd never known him wear anything.

Not in the entire—what?—three and half weeks of their relationship. Hardly a lifetime but, given a choice, it would have been. She'd fallen so hard and so fast for the gorgeous young doctor with the ready smile and sexy, sexy eyes.

Lord, it was laughable how besotted she had been—still was, for heaven's sake! Her husband had walked out, her kids were confused, and all she could think about was him lying there—

'Sal?'

She jumped and turned her head, to see him standing by her car door, safely dressed in jeans and a sweatshirt, the dog on a lead beside him. She opened the window and smiled weakly, feeling the colour seep into her cheeks. 'Hi. I was…' Fantasising about him naked.

'Just passing?' he finished slowly, when she'd run out of words, and she felt the smile collapse.

'Sorry. Bit pathetic today. I couldn't sleep.'

'Me neither. Never can after a night shift. We've just been in the dog park, and I was going to take Scruff to visit Alfie. Want to come? I don't really know the way and I've never met him, but it's on my list of instructions from Annie— "Visit Alfie with Scruff on Saturday at three." So here I am, just about to go and ready for moral support. Going to take pity on me?'

She laughed, as she was meant to, and started to relax. 'He's just an old man,' she teased. 'Why would you need moral support?'

He grinned. 'You wouldn't want me to get into trouble with Annie, would you, now?' he said, and she buckled.

Of course she buckled. And, anyway, it was a perfectly legitimate reason to spend time with him, since she'd known Alfie as one of the A and E regulars for years.

'Your car or mine?' he asked, and then a car pulled up behind her and hooted, and he grinned and waved and ran round to the passenger side and got in. 'Guess that's that sorted,' he said, and settled Scruff between his feet before putting on his seat belt and propping himself against the door to watch her.

It hardly seemed worth arguing. 'Right, pay attention,' she said, 'or you'll need me to show you the way next week as well.'

And he promptly shut his eyes, his mouth quirking. Laughing, she slapped his leg in reproach, feeling the hard, solid muscle of his thigh under her fingers, and his eyes flew open and locked with hers.

She felt the laughter recede, replaced by a sudden heat that took her breath away. Her fingers were still tingling from the contact, but the man behind hooted again, and Scruff whined, and she put the car into gear, dragged her eyes from Jack's and set off down the road with her gaze fixed firmly ahead and her hands clamped on the wheel.

Except to change gear, and then his knee was there, jutting against the gear lever, big and bony and attached to those thigh muscles that she was trying so hard not to think about. If only she'd got an automatic!

Hell's teeth.

The chemistry between them was still every bit as hot as it had ever been, and infinitely harder to ignore now that David had left her and they didn't even have the barrier of her marriage between them. He shifted his knee away from the gear lever and scratched the dog's ears, trying to drag his attention onto something innocuous rather than the nearness of her hand when she changed gear, the movement of her thigh as she depressed the clutch, the faint hint of perfume drifting from her skin.

She turned into a driveway and pulled up in a corner of the car park, then cut the engine and reached for the doorhandle. 'Right, this is it. Did you register the route for next week?'

Not a chance. He hadn't seen a single road sign or junction. His attention had been exclusively on her, but he'd work it out next week if he had to.

'I'll be fine,' he said, a little more tersely than he'd meant to, and opened the car door. With any luck, half an hour with an old codger would settle his libido down again and give him back a little much-needed distance!

'Scruff! Come on, then, boy!'

The dog whined and Jack let him go, watching with a smile as he ran to his old master and hopped up onto his lap, lashing his face with his tongue until Alfie, laughing, had to push him away. Then Scruff curled into a ball on his lap and closed his eyes with a sigh of contentment as Alfie laid a hand on his head and scratched gently behind one ear.

He looked across at them as they approached, a smile lighting his rheumy old eyes as he caught sight of Sally.

'Hello, my dear,' he said, his voice a little rough. 'I wasn't expecting you. What brings you here?'

'You do. Hello, Alfie,' Sally said, and to Jack's surprise—or maybe not—she kissed his grizzled cheek. 'How are you, you old rascal? Behaving yourself?'

'I'll have you know I'm a reformed character, you cheeky minx. And you must be Oz,' he said, his eyes flicking up to Jack's and scanning him assessingly. 'Annie and Patrick told me you'd be looking after the old boy while they were away. Thank you for that.'

'My pleasure,' he said, holding out his hand, and after a moment's hesitation Alfie lifted his hand from the dog's neck and took it, and Jack felt he'd passed a test. He smiled. 'Good to meet you, Alfie. I've heard a lot about you.'

Which wasn't totally true, but he'd heard enough, and one look at the worn old eyes was enough to tell him that a lifetime wouldn't be long enough to learn it all. Alfie's hand was retracted and returned to the dog, as if this weekly contact with Scruff was one of the few pleasures he had left, and yet from what Annie had told him he was happy there and doing well.

'So, how was the wedding?' he asked Sally, and Jack pulled up a couple of chairs while Sally settled down to tell him all about it.

Well, maybe not quite all. There was a dance that didn't get a mention, and David's name was notable by its absence, but if Alfie noticed he didn't say anything, just listened intently and then sighed in contentment.

'Well, I hope they'll be very happy. Lovely people, they are, both of them, and if they're a tenth as happy as me and my missus were, they'll be doing all right.'

'I'm sure they are,' Sally assured him, but at that point Jack stopped listening, his attention drawn to one of the other residents.

She was looking a little peaky, and as he watched she stood up and headed out of the room, pausing in the doorway to steady herself.

'Old Emily over there's been going on all morning about feeling dizzy, but she won't tell anyone,' Alfie said, his own eyes following her progress.

Jack flicked his eyes back to Emily and frowned slightly. She didn't look great at all, and he noticed Sally glance across and frown as well.

'Did you mention it to anyone?' she asked Alfie softly, but he shook his head.

'No—she'd never forgive me. She won't say anything—doesn't want to be a nuisance.'

'I'll go and have a word,' Jack said, straightening up,

but as he did so Emily made a funny little noise and crumpled to the floor.

He crossed the room in three strides, kneeling down beside her and feeling for a pulse, but it was very weak.

'Sally, get help,' he said, and without moving her he tilted her head a fraction to open her airway and checked her pulse again. Still very weak, but maybe a little stronger…

'Emily? Wake up, my love!' he said, pinching her gently, and she opened her eyes and moaned.

'Oh, my leg.'

'Which one, sweetheart?'

'This one.' She used her gnarled old hand to pat the knee of the leg she'd landed on.

'Did it hurt before you fell?'

She shook her head. 'No. Oh, dear, I've done my hip, haven't I?'

'Maybe. I think we ought to get you taken to hospital and checked over. They can take some pictures of it to be certain.'

'I think so,' Sally agreed. 'It's a classic fall for a hip fracture—we have to check.'

'I've called an ambulance,' one of the home staff said, kneeling down beside him on the floor and stroking Emily's hair gently back from her face. 'What made you fall, my darling?'

'Alfie said she's been dizzy,' Sally told her softly.

'Oh, why didn't you say? Silly girl. It's those pills,' she added to them. 'They've changed her blood-pressure pills, and they warned us to keep an eye on her. It was a bit low this morning, and I told her to let me know if she felt funny. Oh, Em, you should have said.'

'I didn't want to be a nuisance,' she said, her eyes filling, and the woman clicked her tongue and gave her a little hug, then sat down with Emily's head on her lap and stroked her hair until the ambulance arrived.

'She all right?' Alfie asked anxiously, when they rejoined him a few minutes later.

'She will be. She might have broken her hip, or it might just have had a bit of a bump. They'll X-ray her and see.'

'You take care of her, now,' Alfie said. 'She's a good woman.' And to Jack's surprise, his wizened old cheeks coloured.

Jack patted his hand. 'Don't worry, she's in good hands,' he promised. 'But if it makes you feel happier, we'll go up to the hospital and check on her.'

'Good. Go now—and let me know?'

'Of course we will, you old softie,' Sally said affectionately, and kissed his still-ruddy cheek. 'Be good, now.'

'Got no choice in here,' he said, but he didn't look unhappy about it, and the dog trotted out with them without a whimper. Good, because Jack had had visions of having to drag the hound after them on the end of his lead, whining all the way.

'Are you really going to the hospital?'

He looked at Sally in surprise. 'Well—yes, I was. I said I would. You don't have to come, though.'

She laughed. 'Oh, I do. I was going anyway. I'm just surprised you are.'

He didn't feel flattered by that, but he didn't argue. He'd done nothing in the past to give her a good opinion of him, unless you counted doing his duty when he'd married Clare, and somehow he didn't think she would.

It was almost six by the time they left the hospital.

Emily was fine, just a little bruised, and they were

keeping her in overnight under observation just to be on the safe side. While Sally had waited with her, Jack had gone to see Jennifer, the woman whose hand he'd amputated in the night, and he came back just in time to hear Sally telling Alfie the news that Emily was going to be OK.

He glanced at his watch and cocked his head on one side enquiringly. 'Hungry?'

She was. Ravenous. She'd missed lunch—had probably missed breakfast, too—and the thought of food made her stomach grumble loudly.

'I take it that's a yes.' He chuckled, and she blushed and nodded.

'I am, but don't worry, I can go home and cook.'

'Well, we can all go home and cook, but we could also pick up a take-away from the Chinese round the corner.' He grinned ruefully. 'Share supper with an old friend who's miles from home?' he said, and her resolution went belly up without a murmur.

She smiled wryly. 'Since you put it like that,' she told him, and picked up her car keys.

He was worried about her. She seemed fine in many ways, but there was a haunted look in her eyes and he knew the boys were troubling her.

Was it only the boys, though? He didn't know, he just knew he hated seeing her like this and wanted to take her out of herself.

'I gave Jennifer her ring,' he told her as they unpacked the bag in the Corrigans' kitchen a little while later.

'How is she?'

He grimaced. 'Sore, shocked, grieving. I told her we'd got the ring for her, and she took it from me and held it helplessly and didn't know what to do with it. She couldn't put it on, of course, and it hit her then, I think, that she'd lost the other arm. I had to help her put it on her finger on her right hand, and it made her cry. She said the last time a man had done that, it had been her husband on their wedding day. It was awful, and there was nothing I could do but let her talk and just be there for her, a total stranger putting on her wedding ring.'

He shook his head, the look in her eyes still tormenting him, and Sal made a soft sound and laid her hand on his. 'It must have been so difficult. I'm sorry, I could have done it instead. It might have been easier—a nurse, another woman. Reminded her less.'

He shook his head. 'I don't think it would have made any difference, so don't be sorry. Anyway, I didn't mind. It's part of the job—the bit that makes us human. It was just sad, that's all. She's got a lot to work through before she comes out the other end—grieving not only for her husband but for her arm. That's a lot of adjusting to make. It won't be a picnic.'

'You saved her, though, so at least she'll get the opportunity. She would have bled out if she'd been left much longer.'

'Oh, yes,' he agreed, 'but this morning I don't think she was grateful to me for that. Maybe in time she'll come to feel she was lucky. Who knows?'

He looked down at her hand, still resting on his, and he could see the white indentation where her wedding ring had been, a poignant reminder of all she'd lost. He reached out with the other hand and traced the white line with his finger, and as if he'd scalded her she sucked in her breath and snatched it back, but he could still feel the warmth of her palm on the back of his hand, still feel the dent where her ring had sat for so long.

'Um—so what did we get in the end, then?' she said, breaking the silence and delving into the bag with forced cheer.

He stared at the bag for a moment, trying to concentrate on something other than the feel of her hand. 'Um… I don't know—it was a set meal for two. Seems a decent place—it's kept me going most of the week, and I haven't found anything yet I don't like.'

She laughed and shook her head. 'That's dreadful—don't you cook at all?'

'Oh, sure. I'm cooking for them tomorrow, but it doesn't seem worth bothering just for me after a long day at work, so I'm used to take-aways. Either that or a bowl of cereal.'

She frowned, as if she couldn't quite make sense of his remark, but the food was getting cold and he was starving. He grabbed a spoon and put it in her hand. 'Come on, it's getting cold.'

So she dug in, and he followed suit, and for the next half-hour they ate and watched pretty much nothing on the television, until in the end the silence between them became too much and he had to break it.

'How are the kids?' he asked, for something to say, and she shrugged.

'I don't know. They were out when I rang at two-thirty.'

So that was why she was unhappy. She was missing her babies, and the nest was just too darned empty. His heart ached for her. He knew just what it felt like to be in an empty nest, and nothing was going to take that away.

Not even time. Time might take the edges off, but then

you just got bruises instead of cuts. There was little to choose between them.

He was just going to have to make sure he didn't add to her problems.

'Coffee?' he offered, but she shook her head.

'No, thanks. I ought to be going. The boys might ring.'

But she didn't get up, and the silence stretched out. 'You could ring them from here,' he suggested, but she shook her head, and she did stand up then, at last, picked up her bag and headed for the door.

He followed her, reached for the latch, looked down into her eyes.

Her mouth was open slightly, as if she was about to speak and had forgotten her lines, and his eyes were drawn to it. Inches. That was all it was. Just mere inches between them, and if they both leaned a little...

'Thank you for today.'

He sucked in a breath and straightened up. 'My pleasure.'

He opened the door, let her out and watched her drive away, then closed the door and dropped his head forwards against it.

His heart was racing, his blood pressure sky high, and if it wasn't for the fact that he didn't know where she lived, he'd follow her home and—

'What? You'd what?' he said roughly. 'Make love to her in the bed she's shared with David for the last however long? She probably hasn't even changed the sheets yet!'

Disgusted at himself, raging with frustration and sick with longing, he went back into the sitting room, gathered up their plates and glasses and put them into the dishwasher, then locked up the house and took Scruff for a brisk walk.

Probably too brisk.

The poor old boy limped gamely along beside him, and he slowed his pace, scratched the dog's head and took the shortest route home.

CHAPTER FIVE

PATRICK, Annie and Katie came back at midday on Sunday, and Jack greeted them with lunch in the oven and a certain amount of trepidation. As far as he knew, Sally hadn't told them about David, and he didn't know how he would or even if it was his place to do so, but in the end Katie took the choice out of his hands.

They piled out of the car, looking full of energy and enthusiasm, and Katie came racing in, talking a mile a minute, her eyes sparkling. They'd spent a week at Centerparcs, just a normal family holiday followed by a couple of days with Annie's parents, but Katie was bursting to share it.

'It was brilliant! It had white-water rapids in the pool and I did archery and we went bowling and it was amazing! We had our own little house in the woods and bikes and there were squirrels every morning right outside—wait till I tell Alex!' she said excitedly. 'Mummy, can I ring him?'

'Hey, your lunch is almost ready and, anyway, he's out for the day,' Jack said quickly. 'Why don't you phone him later, and maybe you could take Scruff out in the garden and play with him while I finish off the cooking. I reckon he's missed you.'

'OK!' She bounced out of the French doors in the dining room with the dog in hot pursuit, and Jack pulled the door closed behind them and turned back to his friends. What to say? There was no easy way to do this, but they had to know so they could deal with Katie.

Patrick, though, took one look at his face and his eyes narrowed. 'What's happened?'

'You might want to ring Sal,' he said softly, directing his words to Annie. 'David's left her.'

Her face paled, and she turned to Patrick, her eyes filled with distress. 'I knew there was something—Oz, did she say why?'

'He's moved in with his PA—Wendy.'

'My God, she joked about it,' Patrick said slowly. 'Is she OK?'

He shrugged. 'Sort of. They're both pretty cut up for the boys, but there has to be a better reason than that to stay together. Kids can tell when things aren't right, and if your heart's not in it there's no point in going on. You have to be happy, too. You have to love each other.'

'They used to,' Annie said. 'I thought.'

'Did they? Really? That wasn't the impression I got, reading between the lines. From what little she's said I don't think they should ever have got married.'

Annie looked at him, looked at Patrick and shook her head. 'No. No, you're right. They were good friends, but there was no sparkle. They weren't happy like us, but I didn't think either of them was looking for that, not after…' She shook her head again, as if she'd been going to add something but had changed her mind. 'I need to see her.'

'Ring her. She should be at home, the kids won't be back till later on.'

'Is it public knowledge?' Patrick asked, and he nodded.

'Sort of. She hasn't broadcast it, but it's a hospital. You don't need to.'

'No,' Annie said drily. 'That's certainly true. I just wonder if the school will know, as they're going back tomorrow.'

He shrugged. 'You'll have to ask her. I don't know if she's told them, she hasn't said.'

'I'll call her now.' Face troubled, Annie left the room, and Patrick turned to him, his eyes searching.

'I take it this is nothing to do with you?'

He raised his hands in the air in surrender. 'Me? How's it possibly to do with me? The man's fallen in love. All I've done is support Sal. I brought her here on Monday and let her sleep for a while on the sofa and fed her, and I fed her last night—we went to see Alfie with the dog and then got a takeaway. Apart from that and work, I haven't spoken to her, I swear. Or touched her,' he added with a dash of sarcasm.

Patrick's mouth tightened. 'I'm glad to hear it,' he said, and Jack felt his temper flare.

'What the hell do you take me for? The poor bloody woman's marriage has just fallen apart!'

Patrick just arched a brow. 'Don't get indignant with me, Oz. It's not as if you two don't have history.'

'That was years ago.'

'And you still love her.'

His temper died down as quickly as it had flared. He looked away, rammed his hand through his hair, swallowed hard. 'Is it that obvious?'

'It was to me, at the wedding—when you were dancing. If you could call it that.'

Jack said something rude under his breath and stalked over to the range cooker. 'I need to check the lunch,' he growled, and yanked the oven door down, glaring at the leg of lamb as if it was personally responsible for his problems.

'Anything I can do?'

'Yes. Keep out of my way and don't make crass insinuations.'

'Hardly insinuations. You were damn near making love to her on the dance floor. A blind man on a galloping horse could see that.'

'It wasn't that bad,' he snapped with a flicker of guilt.

'Oh, it was. If I hadn't been so busy dancing with my own wife I would have cut in to salvage what was left of Sally's reputation—so tell me why I shouldn't be concerned that you'd take advantage of this latest turn of events.'

He snorted and rammed a hand through his hair. 'You must really think I'm a bastard.'

'Oh, get off your high horse, Oz. When did you get so virtuous? You never used to be reticent if you wanted a woman.'

Jack slammed the oven door and spun round. 'I was a student. I was in my early twenties—and I didn't exactly hear them protesting. And anyway, who the hell are you to talk about behaving in public? I can remember the way you used to carry on with Ellie.'

Patrick flinched, and he stopped, appalled at himself, and swore softly but fluently. 'I'm sorry. That was utterly uncalled for. I'm really glad you had that time with her— you deserved it, and I'm just jealous.'

'Jealous? Ellie died!'

'I know—but you were great together, and when I met Sal, I thought maybe we...' He broke off, then went on gruffly, 'But it just didn't happen that way, and now, seeing her again— Oh, hell. Ignore me. I'm frustrated and crabby and I just wish there was a way…'

Patrick was silent for a moment, then he said softly, 'Lord, you really do love her, don't you?' Jack nodded, swallowing the lump in his throat, and Patrick reached out a big hand and rumpled his hair. Usually it annoyed the hell out of him, but this time the contact was curiously welcome. 'I'm sorry. You're right to be angry. I don't know you any more. You've changed—we both have. And if you think this is the real deal, then you'd be crazy not to go for it. You could always stick around,' he added, his voice casual, 'let her get over the initial shock of David leaving—so long as you aren't just messing her around…'

He trailed off, leaving his suggestion hanging in the air as Annie came back in and snuggled into his arms. 'She's OK. She's on a late tomorrow and so am I, so we're going to get the kids off to school and spend the morning together. It won't get the washing done, but who cares? Sally's much more important.' She looked up at Jack with a thoughtful little frown. 'She said you'd been looking after her, Oz. Thank you.'

He nearly laughed out loud. She wouldn't be thanking him if she knew just how close he'd come last night to kissing her—regardless of what he'd just said to Patrick. He wondered if she knew that they had history. Had Sally told her? Or had Patrick? If so, she didn't mention it, and he certainly wasn't going to be the one to do it. Let Sally tell her tomorrow morning if she wanted her to know.

'The lamb's ready,' he said, his voice a little gruff. 'I'll just put the veg on. Go and round Katie up.' And he turned back to the kitchen and let Patrick's words run through his head. *If you think this is the real deal, then you'd be crazy not to go for it. You could stick around, let her get over the initial shock of David leaving—so long as you aren't just messing her around.* What then? Could they take up where they'd left off? Have a future together? And maybe even—

No. That was too much to wish for, and he was getting ahead of himself. Light years. He poured boiling water on the broccoli and cauliflower florets, took the lamb out of the oven to rest and made the gravy while the potatoes finished off. The plates were warmed in the little oven, the table was laid. All they needed was a bottle of wine or a jug of water and they were good to go.

He glanced out of the window and saw Patrick, Annie and the dog out in the garden with Katie. She was on her swing, and Jack felt a pang of regret. She was the same age as Chloe, with the same delightful open personality, and his heart squeezed with loss.

Lord, he missed her. Even though—

'Is it ready, Oz?' Annie called.

He nodded, and Patrick scooped Katie off the swing, giggling and squirming in his arms, and carried her into the kitchen, dumping her in front of the sink.

'Right, wash your hands and come and sit down,' he said, and Jack reached out to stroke her head instinctively, his fingers gliding over the baby-soft hair so like Chloe's. She tipped her head back and smiled at him, and his heart squeezed again.

God, Patrick was a lucky man, but he'd earned his luck the hard way, and he deserved it more than anyone else Jack knew.

It was just a shame there wasn't more to go around.

* * *

'So what happened? It was so sudden.'

Sally shook her head. 'Not really. It's been coming for ages, I was just refusing to see it.' She sat back on the sofa where she'd curled up and slept just a week ago that day, and told Annie all about it. And when she'd finished, and had wiped away the stupid, stupid tears that just wouldn't stay put, she gave a sad little laugh.

'I knew, really—knew in my heart of hearts about Wendy, but also right at the beginning, I knew it wasn't right. We should never have got married.'

'So why did you?'

'Because I was pregnant—you know that.'

'That's never a good enough reason,' Annie pointed out unnecessarily. 'You didn't have to marry him. You could have coped on your own. There has to be more than just security.'

'There was more. And he's been good to us.'

Annie nodded. 'He has—much better than Colin. Colin lied to me for years about the gambling. At least David had the decency not to have an affair with Wendy while he was still with you.'

'Well, so he said, and I think I have to believe him, because if you look at him now, he's quite different and he couldn't have hidden that. He's happy, you know? Deep down inside. He looks like Patrick, deeply content and…not smug, that's the wrong word, but as if everything's all right in his world.'

'And what about yours?' Annie asked searchingly, and Sally's heart did a little flip, because her world was in chaos and the only bright thing in it at the moment apart from her beloved boys was Jack, and she really didn't want to go there. Not after Saturday night when he'd so, so nearly kissed her. She knew exactly where that would have ended, unless his brakes were a sight more effective than hers, and from the look in his eyes she didn't think they would have been.

'I'm OK,' she said quietly. 'And the boys say Wendy is really nice, so it's all going to work out at that end. She's got a little girl called Harriet, and they've all spent lots of time together this week, so the boys are getting to see David for the first time in ages. And at least neither of us have to have headaches at bedtime any more,' she added lightly.

'Oh, Sally.' Annie reached out a hand and touched her on the shoulder, not fooled at all by her feeble attempt at humour. 'I'm so sorry I wasn't here for you. It must have been so awful.'

She shook her head. 'Don't worry, I coped, and Jack was great. He really looked after me.'

'Patrick said…' Annie coloured and broke off, and Sally's heart sank. So she knew. Damn.

'That was years ago,' she said. Even if in her heart it still felt like yesterday. 'And he's been a perfect gentleman. He's kept me focussed and busy at work, so I haven't had time to brood, and he's mopped me up and fed me—he's been a real friend.'

Annie looked as if she would have said something else, but then she changed her mind, to Sally's relief, and moved on.

'So where will you all live?' she asked, switching to the practical.

'David's at Wendy's, and the boys and I are in the house. Well, for now. I don't have to sell it initially, because Wendy's is big enough for all of them at the weekends, but

I don't know if I'll want to keep it long term. We've only been there a year, so I don't have any sentimental attachment to it, and I've got hardly any memories of David in it because in all honesty he's hardly even been there. So we might sell it, or we might not. I'll have to see how we all feel a few months down the line.'

'Good idea. There's no rush, take your time. I was desperate to sell this house after Colin killed himself, but I was trapped in it really because of the state it was in and so I didn't have a choice.'

'And now?'

Annie smiled, her face softening. 'Now I feel that it really doesn't matter any more. It's not the house that's important, it's the people. Patrick's turned it into our home and it feels so different now, so full of love and laughter. And he's wonderful with Katie. They just adore each other, and she's so happy now that she won't mind if we move, which is just as well, because—' She broke off, colouring, then went on, 'Oh, rats, I wasn't going to tell anybody yet, but I can't hide it from you, of all people. We're having a baby.'

'Oh, Annie!' She felt the hot sting of tears, and reached out her arms, hugging her friend hard. 'Oh, I'm so pleased for you. That's fantastic news! When?'

'Eight months—mid-December. I'm six weeks.'

Sally pulled a face. 'Oh, I was sick as a parrot by then with Alex. How are you doing?'

'OK. Oz cooked us a roast yesterday and I wondered if I'd manage to eat it, but it was fine. I don't really want to tell him yet, though. I mean, I know Patrick's known him for years, but I haven't, and I just wanted to hug it to myself for a bit. Well, to me and Patrick.'

'How's he taken it?' Sally said, and Annie laughed.

'He's overjoyed—clucking round me all the time, mind you. He's going to drive me mad, I think, but he's so pleased it's lovely to see. He stood over me while I did the test because he couldn't bear the suspense. We did it while Katie was out with my parents on Saturday morning.'

'Have you told her?'

Annie shook her head. 'Not yet. I want to get past eight weeks, at least, in case I lose it. We'll tell her then.'

'I'll keep it under wraps,' Sally promised. 'Oh, Annie, I'm so pleased for you—and thank you for telling me. It's so lovely to have some *good* news!'

'Thank you,' Annie said softly, her eyes misty. 'I just wish—oh, I don't know. I know David's been kind to you, but now I'm with Patrick and I know what love really is— well, I just wish you could be as happy.'

And again, unbidden, Jack popped into her mind. Jack, who had made her unhappier than anyone or anything in her life, but had also, perversely, given her the greatest joy.

'Maybe one day,' she said, knowing it would never happen and putting it out of her mind before she allowed herself to dream about something so impossible. She looked at her watch and stood up, summoning a bright, cheery smile. 'Right, time to go to work. David's got the boys after school, and they're staying with him for the night, so don't be surprised if he turns up with them in the morning outside the school gates.'

'Thanks for the warning. I don't know if I'll know what to say to him.'

Sally hugged Annie reassuringly. 'Hello would be a good start. Really, Annie, we're both fine about it. It's just a bit of a shock, but it's absolutely the right thing for both of us.'

Well, for David, at least. The thing that was right for her was never going to happen…

Jack was there, of course, right in her line of sight when she went into the department, propping up the wall and, judging by the howls of laughter from the group around him, telling yet another of his outrageous jokes.

She didn't want to smile, but just the sound of his laughter made her want to join in.

No. Pathetic. She was made of sterner stuff than that. She walked briskly down the corridor to the staffroom and hung up her coat, bent down to stash her bag and keys at the bottom of her locker and caught sight of his feet right beside her.

As if she'd needed to see them. The hair on the back of her neck had stood on end the moment he'd walked in.

'Hi,' he said softly, and she chucked her keys at the locker, straightened up and shut it and then turned round with a carefully neutral smile plastered to her face.

'Hi, there. Good weekend?'

He searched her face for a second, then nodded. 'Yes, thanks. You?'

She thought of yesterday, moving her things out of the bedroom she'd shared with David into the guest room, smaller but prettier, overlooking the garden instead of the cul-de-sac at the front, and smiled. 'Fine. I did a bit of turning out. Banishing demons, that sort of thing. Very therapeutic.'

He smiled understandingly. 'Absolutely. Did you see Annie?'

She nodded. 'Yes. I had a coffee with her.'

'Is she still drinking it?'

She opened her mouth, shut it and looked away. 'Of course—why ever not?'

'Just wondered. Most pregnant women go off it.'

So he did know—or he was guessing. She didn't know, and wasn't going to confirm his suspicions if that was all they were, but her hesitation was enough.

'Don't worry,' he murmured, 'I won't say anything till they tell me, but there was just something in her eyes. I guess when you've seen enough pregnant women, you start to recognise it. Like they're hugging a secret.'

'I thought men weren't supposed to be able to read women?' she quipped lightly, and he laughed, a soft ripple of sound that made her hair stand on end all over again.

'Whatever gave you that idea?' he said, and then moved away from her, so she could breathe again. 'I hope you're feeling full of beans, we've got a crowded waiting room and I think Angie wants you on cubicles with me.'

Angie did, or he'd engineered it? Whatever, she didn't mind. She liked being on cubicles, and there'd be a lot she could do without involving him.

Or so she'd thought. Of course, her first patient needed his attention immediately, and she wasn't sure if that was a good thing or not. Sure, working with him was deeply unsettling, but it made her feel so *alive*, in a way she hadn't felt for years.

Getting on for ten, in fact.

And she needed him now because Mrs Roper, a delightful lady in her mid-seventies, had fallen onto her outstretched hand and given herself a classic Colles' fracture.

She was wheeled in by her neighbour, her arm propped on a pillow. 'Oh, dear, that looks sore,' Sally said, crouching down and rearranging the pillow to give better support.

'I've broken it, haven't I?' she said with a sigh, and Sally looked at the distorted limb and nodded.

'I'm afraid so. But don't worry, we can fix it. Let me just check your details, Mrs Roper.' She ran through the form, then stood up and patted her shoulder gently. 'Right. You just sit here for a minute and I'll get a doctor to come and see you. I won't be long.'

She stuck her head round the curtain and caught Jack just as he was heading down the corridor. 'Got a minute? I've got a Colles' for you.'

'Oh, great, I love a good Colles'.' He changed direction and came in, rubbing his hands with gel, and smiled at their patient. 'Hi. I'm Jack Logan, one of the doctors here. And you've had a nasty tumble. Ouch.'

'Mrs Roper's fallen down the last few stairs at home and landed on the hall floor,' Sally supplied, and she nodded confirmation.

'It was so silly—I'd put the washing there to go upstairs and then forgotten to take it, and of course when I came down, I found it! I'm so cross.'

'Don't be cross. We all do stupid things. The most important thing to do is check out the circulation in your hand before we do anything else.' He pressed her nails and watched them pink up again instantly, and nodded in satisfaction. 'So far, so good. When did you last eat?'

'Breakfast. I was just coming down to make lunch—and the last time I was asked that, I was about to have an operation,' she said, eyeing him dubiously.

He smiled. 'It's possible you may need one,' he agreed. 'You won't if I have my way, but we do need to do a procedure called a Bier's block to numb it so I can line the bones up without hurting you, and then we can plaster it, but first of all we need X-rays so we know just what we're dealing with. If Sally gets that organised, I'll come back and see you with the results. Don't worry, we'll get you sorted and home again as soon as we can.'

And with a cheerful wink and a grin, he disappeared, leaving Mrs Roper with the sort of besotted smile that Sally felt creeping onto her own face all too often when she was in his company.

Except that today she didn't feel like smiling, because before he'd left the cubicle he'd caught her eyes and it was there again, that latent heat, just waiting for an opportunity to flare into life.

No way. He was far too dangerous to her fragile status quo.

On autopilot, she took Mrs Roper for her X-rays, called Jack once the films were ready and then helped him prepare her for the procedure.

The tourniquet cuff was slipped onto her arm high up, over some soft padding, and he checked the pulse in her wrist, then slid a small cannula into the back of her hand, making her wince a little. 'Sorry, I know it's sore,' he murmured. 'Soon be more comfy. Right, that's looking good. Sal, if you could hold Mrs Roper's arm up there for me—that's lovely,' he said, and while Sally held the arm up and kept pressure on the brachial artery to prevent the blood from refilling the arm, Jack told Mrs Roper what they were doing and why, and put a cannula in the other arm.

'Just in case we need to give you any other drugs at any time,' he explained, 'because there's a very slight chance your body might not like the local anaesthetic, and then we can give you something to counteract your reaction to it without messing about.'

She arched one fine, autocratic brow. 'Is that really a possibility, or are you just covering all your bases so I don't sue?' she asked, and he chuckled.

'A bit of both. You have to give informed consent, and you can't if you aren't informed, but sometimes you can frighten the living daylights out of your patients and then they won't let you give them the treatment they need. It's a bit of a tightrope.'

'Just so long as you don't fall off it halfway through doing my arm,' she said, her smile returning, and he taped down the cannula and grinned.

'Oh, I'm very good at walking tightropes,' he said, flicking a glance at Sally. 'How are you doing there? Thumb OK?'

She nodded. Actually her thumb was beginning to burn from pressing down on the artery, but the limb was pale and the tourniquet cuff was ready to be inflated.

'Ready to go?'

She nodded again, and he patted Mrs Roper's other hand. 'Right. Let's get the local in and give it a few minutes to take effect, and then we can get your arm looking the right shape again.'

'Oh, that'll be good. It is a bit weird.'

'Rather fetching. It'd stop your handbag from sliding off your arm,' he said, teasing a laugh from her, and he kept the lightweight banter up as he injected the local into the cannula, but even though he was laughing and joking with her, Sally knew he was watching Mrs Roper very carefully for any sign of an adverse reaction.

She was lying on a tipping trolley now in case, but she was fine, and while Sally kept an eye on the pressure in the tourniquet cuff to make sure it didn't fall, he checked her wrist to see if it was numb. Once he was happy that she wouldn't feel any pain, he took her hand and, with Sally holding her arm steady, stretched it out to pull the fracture into line, bent her hand down a little and swivelled it out to the side, relieving the pressure on the impaction and restoring her arm to a much more normal appearance.

'There, that's better. You've lost your handbag rest now.'

Mrs Roper chuckled weakly and peered at it, then lay back against the pillows. 'Oh, I feel all funny. I never realised I was so squeamish.'

Jack's eyes sharpened, and his eyes flicked to the cuff monitor.

'Cuff pressure's fine,' Sally said softly, checking Mrs Roper's blood pressure in the other arm simultaneously and nodding. 'BP's a little lower.'

'OK. Keep talking to me, sweetheart. How are you feeling now?'

'Woozy,' she said.

'Any ringing in your ears, or numbness in your lips and tongue?'

She shook her head. 'No. I just felt a bit faint. I think I'm not as brave as I thought I was. It's better now.'

Jack nodded and rested a hand on her knee. It could have been a comforting gesture, but Sally knew he was feeling for any muscle twitching or tremor as well as offering reassurance.

'Better now?' he asked after a moment or two, and she nodded and smiled.

'I'm sorry. How silly of me.'

'I don't think so. You've been through a lot. Still, we'll just keep an eye on you for a little while, and then once we're sure you're OK we'll take the cuff off in about half an hour to give the anaesthetic time to disperse into your tissues, then once we're really happy we'll get a little cast on there to hold it in place until tomorrow.'

'What happens then?'

'You need to come back and have a check-up in the fracture clinic, and if it's all fine you can have a proper cast on.'

'And if not?'

'Then we'll think again, but it's in a pretty good position now. We'll just check it with another set of X-rays while it's still numb, and then we can put the back-slab on.'

He checked the new set of plates, nodded his satisfaction with the alignment, monitored her carefully during the deflation of the cuff and handed her over to Sally for a back-slab.

Because of the risk of delayed toxicity, Sally kept a very close eye on her during the procedure and for another hour afterwards, leaving the curtain open and popping in and out every few minutes. Her daughter arrived, having driven up from London, and Sally felt happier that she had someone with her to take her home and look after her for the first few hours at least. Once she was sure the danger of reaction was passed, she got Jack to sign Mrs Roper off and sent her on her way with her daughter.

'We'll see you tomorrow, and you take care,' she said with a smile. 'Don't forget to take your painkillers—there's no need to be brave.'

'Oh, I'll take them, don't worry. It's beginning to feel a little sore now.'

'It will. Keep the sling on as much as possible, and rest it on your lap on a pillow when you're sitting down, and just take it easy—and don't put the washing on the stairs!' she teased.

'Oh, no chance of that! It's going straight into the drawers the moment I get her home,' her daughter said firmly.

Sally waved them off, and turned to find Jack by the central desk, watching her.

'Teabreak?' he suggested, and she glanced at her watch and realised with amazement that it was almost four.

'I'll just grab a cold drink,' she said. 'The waiting room's heaving and it'll only get worse once everyone knocks off from work.'

He nodded, and she thought he'd leave it at that, but he followed her to the staffroom and poured two glasses of squash, handing her one. 'Nice lady, Mrs Roper. Everything OK? Were you happy with her?'

'I think so. I think it was just a little faint.'

'So do I, but I wanted to be sure. Sorry it took so long.'

'It's hardly your fault I had to monitor her.' And anyway, it hadn't been a hardship. Mrs Roper at least was polite and grateful, unlike some of their customers. Spending a few hours with her knocked spots off Friday nights in the easiness stakes.

She glanced back at Jack, just as he tipped his head back to drain his glass, and as she watched his throat work she had to trap the tiny moan of need that rose in her chest. No. Stop it. Too dangerous…

'Right, back to work, I suppose,' he said, putting the glass down, and she poured the rest of hers away and rinsed them both out. Anything rather than look at him and risk him seeing the expression in her eyes.

* * *

The rest of the shift was manic.

Her few peaceful hours with Mrs Roper seemed a million miles away, and she ended up working with Jack in Resus on an RTA victim with severe multiple trauma.

He was finally stable enough for Theatre, and as they sent him off Jack turned to her with a rueful grin. 'What was that you said about it getting worse?' he murmured, and she laughed briefly.

'Sorry. I'll keep my mouth shut in future. Right, it's knocking off time, I'm going home.'

'Me, too. I'll just go and talk to the relatives for a moment, and I'll be off. I'll see you tomorrow.'

If only.

She went into the staffroom, opened her locker and found her bag and coat, but there was no sign of her keys. She pulled out the few things that were in there, but they weren't there, so she searched the area around her locker, even looking in the gap at the end in case they'd fallen down there, but they hadn't.

So where...?

'Problem?'

'I can't find my keys,' she said. 'I had them this morning, I know I did. There's no sign of them, but I put them in my locker like I always do.' Or had she? No. She'd lobbed them at her locker, because he'd appeared silently out of nowhere the moment she'd arrived and totally flummoxed her, but if she'd missed...

'If I give you a lift home, can you get in?'

'Yes—we've got a spare key hidden behind a plant pot.'

'Well, let's go, then, before another emergency comes in and we get sucked in again. You can look for them tomorrow.'

'And how do I get to work? I have to be here at seven.'

'I'll pick you up.'

But then he'd know where she lived.

Stupid. It was hardly a secret, and he'd only got to ask Patrick or Tom, and they'd tell him. And it wasn't like he was a stalker or anything weird.

So she gave in and thanked him, and they walked back to Patrick and Annie's street, got into his car and she directed him to her house.

He turned onto the drive, pulled up and sat there, engine idling, waiting for her to get out. She should have done it, should have thanked him and opened the door and gone inside, but she didn't. Instead, she opened her mouth and said, 'Do you want something to eat?'

He turned his head and looked at her, his eyes unreadable in the dark. 'Thanks. That would be good,' he said, and cut the engine.

Then it dawned on her just what she'd done.

CHAPTER SIX

He must be crazy.

If he'd had the slightest grain of sense he'd have driven off and left Sally here, but curiosity about her house and life and a ridiculous urge to flagellate himself further with her inaccessibility had him following her in through the door.

It was a new, 'executive-style' house on a small, select development tucked in behind a row of older houses, the sort of thing that most people would be delighted to own, and Jack was amazed at how much he hated it. It was so neutral. Characterless, almost. Not at all the sort of chaotic, warm, loving house he'd pictured her in all these years.

Not that there was anything wrong with the house itself. At first glance it seemed a good house, solidly built and well proportioned, but there seemed no personality about any of it—until he followed her into the kitchen and saw the kids' drawings pinned on the walls, little messages to her held on the fridge with magnets.

'Mum, please wash PE kit. Love you. Alexxxxxx'

A tiny drawing on a sticky note, with 'Best mum' carefully written on the corner and a picture of someone that could have been Sally. Long, dark hair and skirt, big smile and lots of hearts all around it. Different writing, so Ben, then, and saying so much in so few words. He wondered if it was new, generated by recent events, and his heart ached for them all.

'What do you fancy? I've got eggs and potatoes and salad stuff, so I could do an omelette and salad, or egg sandwiches, or I might have a jar of pasta sauce and some mince in the freezer...'

'Omelette sounds lovely,' he said. Quick, too, so he could get out of there before he did something stupid.

'Sit yourself down—do you fancy a glass of wine? There's some white open in the fridge, or there might be a can of lager, or I can make tea or coffee?'

'I'd better make it tea,' he said, erring belatedly on the side of caution. The last time he'd had anything to drink around her he'd nearly seduced her on the dance floor. 'Don't let me stop you if you want wine, though,' he added, and she laughed—a little nervously?

'Oh, I won't. You can pour me a glass of wine and make your tea while I get the meal. Here, the mugs and tea and everything are all above the kettle, and the wineglasses are in the next cupboard along.'

Good idea. Give him something to do apart from watching her swift, economical movements as she walked around the kitchen retrieving ingredients from the fridge and cupboards.

He sat at the table, wondering which of the chairs had been David's and deliberately picking one he thought would have been one of the boys'.

'Nice house,' he said, testing her reaction, and she gave a tiny hollow laugh.

'I'm utterly indifferent to it,' she said. 'It was a ridiculous amount of money and it's not at all the sort of house

I wanted, but David liked it because it was well built and low maintenance.'

Interesting. And none of his business. 'So what did you want?' he asked, ignoring his own advice.

'Something old. Victorian, probably, but not on the same scale as Fliss and Tom's—have you seen it yet?'

He shook his head, and she continued, 'It's amazing. Huge, but, then, it needs to be, they've got six children and his parents and two dogs and several cats and any number of chickens and ducks.'

He laughed. 'Sounds like Fliss.'

'Mmm. I think Tom was a bit bemused at first, but he's got used to it now. But, anyway, something rather more sensible than that, possibly Edwardian. A little detached house with a pretty garden and some lovely original features. Something with character, for heaven's sake, because this is just so bland.'

'So will you move?'

She stopped chopping and stirring, and looked at him steadily for a moment. 'I don't know,' she said slowly. 'I don't want to unsettle the boys any more, and there's plenty of time for my dream house. I expect we'll stay here for a few years.'

'You can put character in.' That was certainly true. He'd seen mud huts with more character, but he didn't put it quite so bluntly.

Her smile was a little sad. 'Mmm. I know.'

So why hadn't she? Was it because her heart had never really been in it, because it was the sort of thing one ought to discuss with a partner, and they never had? Never sat poring over colour charts or furniture catalogues, been to junk sales and come home with something silly—not that he'd had that with Clare, either, but he knew the way it worked in theory. He was still waiting for a chance to put it into practice.

She put the plates down on the table. 'Here—do you want salad cream or mayo? Or I've got a really nice balsamic vinegar.'

'Sounds good,' he said, and she handed him the bottle and sat down at right angles to him, which meant that her leg brushed his as she pulled her chair in.

She mumbled an apology and hitched it out of the way, and he moved his own across into more neutral territory before it got him into trouble, because one more touch and he was going to explode.

'This is lovely, thank you,' he said, piling in and trying not to think about her legs, but it didn't work, and minutes later he was treated to the smooth curve of her bottom as she bent over to put their plates in the dishwasher.

Damn.

He looked away, staring down into his mug, and she came back and reached for it just as he did.

Their fingers clashed and she pulled away, then stopped, leaving her fingertips against his hand, and he let the mug go and turned his hand over, catching her fingers and rubbing them gently between finger and thumb.

'Are you OK? Really?' he asked softly.

She pulled her hand away then and took his mug. 'Yes, I'm fine. The schedule takes a bit of juggling, but it's nothing I can't cope with.'

She put the mug in the dishwasher, her work trousers pulling taut over that soft, lush curve again, and he stood up abruptly and picked up his keys from the worktop and rammed them in his pocket.

'I'd better be off,' he said, and she straightened up and nodded and followed him to the door, looking a little relieved.

'Thank you for the lift—I'll see you in the morning. Quarter to seven OK?'

'Fine. Thanks for the supper.'

'My pleasure.'

And then, just because it seemed the obvious thing to do, because he couldn't help himself another moment and one tiny kiss couldn't hurt, surely, he took half a step towards her, leant over and brushed a kiss against her lips.

Her breath hissed against his lips, and she tilted her head up to his, and he was lost.

Oh, lord, it had been so *long*!

His lips were firm and full and coaxing, not that she needed any coaxing, and he didn't move, just stood there, with his body slightly out of reach, and touched her only with his mouth.

Little sips, tiny nibbles, achingly tender sighs, until she couldn't stand it any longer and moved into his arms.

The heat erupted inside her, ripping through her, tearing a little sob of need and desire from her throat, and he groaned against her mouth and hauled her closer. 'Sal,' he rasped, his breath rough against her cheek, her throat, her chest...

The zip on her tunic gave way to his trembling fingers, and then they were there, cupping one breast and squeezing it as his lips closed hotly over the other, suckling deeply through the fine lace of her bra until she nearly screamed.

Her fingers threaded through his hair, one minute pressing him closer, the next dragging his head up so she could kiss him again, feel his lips on hers, his tongue plundering her mouth as his hands slid down and cupped her bottom and dragged her hard against him.

She arched into him, sobbing with frustration and need, and pulled his shirt out of his trousers, flattening her palms against the hot, smooth skin of his back, feeling the columns of muscle jerk beneath her hands as she slid them down beneath his belt, her fingers flexing into the taut globes of his buttocks.

His groan ripped through her, one hand spearing through her hair, anchoring her head as his mouth plundered hers, his tongue delving, thrusting in time to his hips.

And then without warning he stopped, pulling back, easing away from her, his breath coming hard and fast against her face as he stood just inches away from her. His eyes were black with desire, his lips drawn back, his chest heaving.

'What the hell are we doing?' he grated, and took a step back, then another, then, yanking the door open, he strode out into the night, leaving her speechless.

She sagged against the wall, her fingers coming up to touch her lips. They trembled against the soft, bruised flesh, still moist from his kiss, and her body burned to finish what he'd started.

She heard his car start, heard the gravel skid beneath his wheels, then the squeal of tyres as he tore off down the road. Moving on autopilot, she closed the door and rested her head against it, her heart pounding. What had they been thinking about? If he hadn't stopped—and just then she hated him for that—then they would have been making love right now, right there, in the hall, up against the front door, with her dragging his clothes from his body...

With a whimper of shame she turned away from the door and headed for the kitchen on legs like jelly. She opened the fridge, took out the wine, looked at it and poured it down the sink. The last thing she needed was any more—ever again! One glass! One miserable, pathetic little glass. That was all it had taken to weaken her resolve.

What resolve? she mocked herself. She *had* no resolve where he was concerned. She never had had. Even when Clare had found them together, and he'd gone off to talk to her and come back to tell Sally that he was leaving, marrying Clare because of the baby—even then she'd begged him to make love to her one last time, dragged his clothes off him, clung to him as if she'd die without him. She'd had no pride, no restraint, no dignity. Just desperation—and the consequences of that desperate moment had been immeasurable.

It had taken her *years* to come to terms with it. If she even had. There was no way she was letting it happen again. She was too vulnerable to him, too weak, too much in love…

'Oh, no.' She sat down hard, tears spilling from her eyes, scalding her cheeks. 'No. Not again.'

No, she realised. Not again—still. She'd always loved him, but it was so complicated. She couldn't let this muddy the waters, because there was too much still unresolved, and there probably always would be, and it was only a matter of time before he went back to the other side of the world to his wife and child.

The phone rang, and she stared at it in horror. The children! She'd forgotten to ring to say goodnight.

'Sally? It's David—I just wondered if everything was all right. The kids wanted to stay up to talk to you, but I told them you'd probably had to stay on late.'

'Um—yes, I did,' she said, hating herself for the lie but then adding to it. 'I've only just got in. I'm sorry. Are they asleep?'

'Ben is—Alex is here. Want to talk to him?'

Alex. Oh, lord. 'Sure—put him on,' she said, and took a steadying breath.

'Mum?'

'Hi, darling. Sorry I didn't ring, I was busy. How was your day?'

'OK. Mum, there's a walk this weekend—can we go? Katie said she'd try and get her mum and Patrick to take her, and it would be loads of fun. And Michael and Abby are going, too.'

'OK. I'll find out about it and see if it fits with my work. Maybe your father could take you?'

'But I want *you* to!' he said, and there was a tremor in his voice that nearly broke her heart.

'All right. I'll fix it,' she promised, hoping she could. And she listened to his voice telling her he loved her, and they said goodnight, and only after she'd cradled the phone did she realise that the tears were still streaming down her cheeks...

Jack pulled up round the corner, cut the engine and dropped his head back against the headrest. He was shaking all over, his body screaming for release, aching to hold Sally, to touch her, to plunge deep inside her and lose himself.

How could it still be the same, after so long? He'd been just as desperate before, frenzied every time he'd touched her, unable to resist her or get enough of her. Even when he'd gone back to tell her he was marrying Clare and she'd begged him to make love to her one last time, he hadn't had the strength to walk away.

That much, then, was different. He had the strength now, ten years later, but was it courage or cowardice? She was married still, she had two lovely kids—was he just afraid of the repercussions of such a messy relationship? It was nothing to do with common decency, because where Sally was concerned there was nothing decent about his thoughts. Patrick had been right to distrust him. So much for taking it easy, giving her time to get over the shock— clearly he couldn't be trusted to keep his hands to himself, and it had only been his last shred of self-control that had got him out of there before he'd taken her right there up against the front door.

Jack groaned at the thought, cursing himself for that shred of control and yet knowing that without it he could never have looked Patrick in the eye again.

It might have been a price worth paying.

He was there in the morning at a quarter to seven, as agreed, sitting in the car outside with the engine running and a face like stone.

Sally slid into the seat beside him and fastened her seat belt. 'I didn't know if you'd be here,' she said warily, and he made a sound halfway between a snort and a sigh.

'I said I would.'

'I know, but—' She broke off, wondering about the etiquette of the morning after the night that wasn't. 'We shouldn't have done that,' she said abruptly, and this time it definitely was a snort.

'We didn't do *that*.'

She blushed and shook her head. 'Almost. And it was wrong.'

'Why?'

'Why?' She stared at him in astonishment. 'You tell me—it was you who stopped, not me. You must have had your reasons. Maybe it was something to do with marriage vows,' she added, just a little pointedly.

His mouth tightened, and he slammed the car into gear, dropped the clutch and shot forwards without another word. It wasn't until they turned into the hospital and he pulled up in the car park that he spoke again, his voice stiff and formal.

'You're right, of course. I apologise. I shouldn't have touched you. And don't worry, it won't happen again.'

The sense of regret was shocking.

'Hello, Mrs Roper. How are you?'

'Oh, a bit sore,' she said, smiling bravely, and Jack returned her smile, trying not to notice Sally standing there in the background in what should have been a totally sexless uniform but instead was enough to drive him wild.

Focus, man, focus!

He checked her hand for warmth, for swelling, for sensation, for motor control. Happy that all was well, he gave her the lecture on keeping it moving and asked Sally to put a proper cast on it.

But there must have been something in his voice because as Sally led her away to the plaster room he overheard Mrs Roper say, 'He doesn't seem very happy today—have you two had a fight?'

And Sally straightened her spine and said, 'No, of course not. I expect he's just a bit preoccupied about another patient.'

'Of course. I'm sorry, you have so many people to care for, you really didn't need me being so silly and doing this.'

He walked off, a little perturbed that Mrs Roper had noticed the atmosphere between them. And if Mrs Roper had noticed, what chance did he have of fooling Patrick?

None.

He had to sort it out with Sally, and as soon as they both had a natural break, he collared her.

'Coffee.'

'No, thanks.'

'Yes. We need to talk.'

'Is there anything to say?'

'Plenty, but not here. Come on, I'll treat you.'

She made a derisory noise, but she went with him, and he took her to the little canteen at the back of the hospital, tucked away miles from the main clinics and so little frequented by patients. Although patients might have been better than colleagues, less nosy, but they were lucky for once and didn't see anyone they knew.

She found a table, and he collected their drinks and a couple of sticky Danish pastries, carried them over to the window and sat down opposite her.

'Did you get your keys back, by the way?' he asked, stalling, but it didn't work.

'Yes. Nice try. What did you want?'

He handed her a cup and smiled warily. 'I just wanted to sort things out a bit. I shouldn't have kissed you last night, it was stupid and unforgivable and rash, and it wasn't fair, but I did and we have to move on. Which Danish do you want?'

She stared at him blankly for a moment, then collected

herself, looked down at the pastries and took the chocolate one, as he'd anticipated. He picked up the other plate.

'So what do you suggest?' she asked, biting into the pastry and nearly sending his blood pressure off the scale.

He dragged his eyes away. 'A truce. No more kisses, no more touches, just getting on with our work and being friends. It's only for another two weeks—less than that. We can do it, Sal. If Mrs Roper's noticed, what the hell do you think Patrick and Annie will make of it? They'll give us both hell.'

She sighed and bit the pastry again. 'There's no way we can fool them.'

'We don't have to fool them. We just have to have nothing to hide. It was a one-off. We can be friends, Sal. I *want* to be friends. You need friends at the moment, and I'm more than happy to do anything I can to help you. Helping with the garden, running around after the kids...'

'That isn't necessary,' she said, a little too fast, and he sighed inwardly. OK, so she didn't trust him with the kids. Yet. She would, though, if he had anything to do with it. All he had to do was prove that he could be a good friend instead of a louse of a lover.

Things were different after that.

He gave her a little more space at work, and although she wouldn't—couldn't!—let him come round while the kids were there, they had an activity evening at school on Thursday evening and he did come and give her a hand with the grass before she had to go and pick them up.

And by Friday, when they had a couple of nasty fractures back to back and she paged Patrick to come down to the department to see them, she wasn't worried about him sensing any tension between her and Jack because their relationship was much more relaxed.

Anyway, she needed to talk to him. She'd discovered that her rota would allow her to go on the walk, because she was on a late on Saturday and not working again until Monday morning, and she'd been meaning to liaise with Patrick and Annie about it, but what with one thing and another—namely, avoiding them because of Jack!—she hadn't got round to it.

So that gave her something positive to talk about rather than an unstructured conversation that left room for probing questions. She met Patrick as he came into the department and took him to the first patient, a young man with a badly mangled leg following a fall from a motorbike. He greeted him with customary warmth, checked the circulation in his foot and told him he'd be taking him up to Theatre later that day to pin and plate the tib and fib, and upped his pain relief.

'I'll see you upstairs later,' he said, and then ushered Sally out. 'So how are things at home?' he asked, and she managed a smile.

'Oh, OK. Ben's been a bit clingy, and Alex is trying his best but I think he's a bit insecure, too. They want to go on this walk on Sunday. I gather you're all going?'

'Yes—Annie was going to phone you but she's been a bit rough with the old sickness.'

'Oh, poor thing. I remember it well,' she said with a pang of guilt that she hadn't rung to ask how she was, but she'd just been so afraid of the searching questions…

'Well, anyway, she's still determined to go, says the fresh air will do her good, and she's got your boots out and been walking round to the shops in them every evening to get her feet used to them.'

Sally laughed. 'They were dreadful after the last one,' she said, and Patrick smiled wryly.

'I know. I remember it well. That was when I met her, on that walk. Love at first hobble.'

She laughed again. 'Tell her I'll make the picnic so she doesn't have to think about food. I'll do it before I come to work tomorrow, and then I won't have to worry about it on Sunday morning, because I won't get finished here till late tomorrow night.'

He pulled a face. 'Rather you than me, Saturday night in A and E.'

'Only till nine, it's not the red-eye.'

'Oz is working Saturday—you'll probably end up side by side again.'

Her heart kicked against her ribs. 'What, just for a change?' she said lightly, but maybe not lightly enough, because Patrick stopped her with a hand on her arm and looked down at her with worried eyes.

'Are you OK working with him?' he asked softly. 'Because if not, I'm sure Tom can manage without him.'

She found a smile. 'I'm fine,' she said. 'He's easy to work with. We make a good team.'

'You talking about me again?'

Patrick rolled his eyes. 'Oz, your ego is phenomenal.'

'But warranted.' He flashed a cheeky grin at his friend and winked at Sally, turning her stomach upside down. 'Or am I wrong?'

'Not on this occasion,' Patrick conceded with a tolerant grin. 'Actually, we were talking about the walk on Sunday.'

'Oh, yeah. I'm looking forward to that,' he said.

'You're coming?' Sally asked, startled, and he threw her a smile that sent her heart all over the place again.

'Oh, yes—wouldn't miss it for the world. I love country rambles.'

He was coming on the walk?

'Good. You can carry the backpack with the picnic in it,' she retorted. 'I'll leave you two to your fractures,' she added, and took herself off, because she suddenly had something much more significant to worry about...

'So, we make a good team, eh?'

His grin was cheeky and his eyes were glinting with mischief. She passed him the printout from the ECG and tried to suppress her answering smile. 'One day you'll overhear something you won't like if you keep eavesdropping,' she told him briskly, and he chuckled.

'That'll make a change.'

He frowned at the printout, nodded and went into the cubicle.

'Right, Mr Gray, it looks like you've had a bit of a heart attack, so let's see if we can't get you more comfortable and then we'll move you down to CCU so they can keep an eye on you for a few days. Can I have ten of morphine, Sal, and we'd better give you something to stop you feeling sick.' He slid a cannula home with ridiculous ease, taped it in place and straightened up.

'I thought it was a heart attack,' Mr Gray said quietly.

'People usually do if it comes on when they're exerting themselves. I think if it happens when you're sitting down you might be more likely to think it was indigestion.'

'My wife said it could be that, but I don't think she really believed it. She'll be worried sick when she finds out. She's such a worrier.'

'Well, she was right to worry this time and call the ambulance, but you're in safe hands now,' Jack said, his voice firm and reassuring, and Mr Gray relaxed visibly, even though he was still in pain.

Sally handed him the drugs to check and gave them to Mr Gray, then once he was more comfortable she called a porter and escorted him down to CCU and left him there. She was tempted to sneak a coffee while she was out, but it was nearly time for her evening break and she was hungry. She'd wait a little and have coffee with her meal in a while. Always assuming she had time for it.

Perhaps she should just grab her break now while the going was good and have a sandwich or something quick.

'Skiving off?'

She jumped, her hand flying up to her chest, and she slapped his arm in mock annoyance. 'Do you creep out of the walls or what?'

He chuckled and fell into step beside her. 'I was just coming to look for you. It's quiet—I thought we could sneak a quick break while the going's good.'

No wonder they made such a good team—she was sure he could read her mind! Either that or they thought alike.

'It'll have to be very quick,' she said repressively, as much to herself as him, and he nodded.

'I only had in mind a coffee and a sandwich. I thought I'd get something more later.'

Alike indeed.

They fell into step, sat down with their snacks and ate quickly in silence, but it was a companionable silence, and if he hadn't stretched out his leg and brushed against hers, it might have been quite innocent.

As it was, her breath caught, she pulled her leg away as he muttered an apology, and the heat was back as if it had never been gone. She looked at her watch and drained her coffee.

'We need to get back.'

'Mmm.'

He stood up, gulping down the last mouthful of his coffee and heading for the door, eating the last half of his second sandwich as he went. She hurried after him, wondering where the fire was, and then noticed the muscle working in his jaw.

So much for relaxed!

CHAPTER SEVEN

DAMN, this was so much harder than he'd expected.

One touch! Just one lousy touch of her leg against his and he was burning up. Friends, hell. He didn't want to be friends with her. He want to touch her, hold her, kiss her all over, plunder all that wonderful soft womanliness, bury himself inside her...

He waved his tag in front of the sensor, slapped the door out of the way and strode up to the whiteboard. 'OK, who wants me first?' he asked, and there was a chorus of cheeky remarks from the nurses.

He found a grin, grabbed the first set of notes he was handed and went into the cubicle. There was a little girl with a cut on her head, and she was burrowing into her mother's lap and sobbing while the blood oozed steadily from the wound.

Good. A nice, quiet little case that would calm and soothe him as effectively as it would his young patient.

'Hello, Megan. I'm Jack,' he said, dropping down onto his haunches and smiling at the little mite. She looked at him briefly, turned her head back into her mother's chest and wailed. Oops. Do something about that smile, Jack, my boy. He tried again, this time on Megan's mother. 'I'm going to have to work on my technique with women,' he said, and she gave a ragged laugh and relaxed.

'Want to tell me what happened?' he asked, and she sighed.

'One of those stupid things. They were arguing about bedtime, and whose turn it was to go first, and she ran away from her brother and tripped and hit her head on the door catch. It was just so quick.'

'It always is with kids. One minute it's fine, the next it's World War Three. Right, Megan, sweetheart, how about letting me have a look at that head? I bet your brother's never had a cut as good as that one.'

The little face emerged from the safety of her mother's chest for a moment and regarded him seriously. 'He broke his arm.'

Clearly a major scoop. 'Did he? Bet it didn't bleed.'

She shook her head and sat up a little straighter. Good. He was getting somewhere. 'Mind if I have a look?'

She tipped her head towards him a little, but he could still hardly see. He parted her hair really gently, but it was too much and her lip wobbled and she turned back to her mother.

'Can you hold her head for me?' he asked softly, but her mother suddenly started to shake, and he put a hand on hers over Megan's knee, and gave her a smile.

'Don't worry. I'll get someone to hold her for you.'

'I can hold her,' the nurse with him said, but he shook his head. The nurse was sweet, but she was young, inexperienced and almost certainly didn't have children. And he wanted someone who knew how to hold a fractious, frightened child.

'It's OK, I'll get Sally to do it this time,' he said. 'Maybe you could find her for me—and tell her we'll need glue.'

'OK.'

'Glue?' Megan's head emerged from her mother again. 'Are we doing sticking?'

'Sort of,' he said, sitting back on his haunches so he wasn't quite so close. 'It's like superglue.'

'Toby got it on his fingers once and had to come and be 'solved off.'

He nodded, trying not to chuckle. 'Sounds about right.'

'Want me?'

He turned his head and looked up at Sally, her tunic touching her lush curves in all the right places, and he felt heat rip through him again. Want her? With bells on.

'I need you to help me with Megan. Her mum needs to stretch her legs for a minute, and we need to stick the little cut on her head back together, but I want someone to help me hold that beautiful hair out of the way so I don't get glue in it and ruin it.'

'Oh, no, you don't want to do that. It would be such a shame, it's such pretty hair.' She dropped down beside Megan and smiled softly. 'I tell you what, if you sit on my lap like you are on your mum's while she goes for a walk just up and down out here, then I can hold your hair very, very still, and you can lean on me so you don't move at all, and Jack can stick the little cut.'

She shook her head. 'It's a big cut,' she insisted, and Sally smiled.

'Actually, it is *quite* a big cut,' she agreed, and Megan looked just a tiny bit victorious.

'Her brother's had a broken arm, but it didn't bleed,' Jack offered, helping her out—not that he thought she needed it. Her eyes were like saucers. Talk about the art of coarse acting!

'Didn't it?' she said incredulously, and Megan giggled and shook her head.

'Mine's better,' she said, but Jack wondered how much that would help once her mother disappeared and Sally had to hold her still for his gluing.

'I tell you what, let's get you all fixed, and then I can find some other stickers and we can put them on you—would you like that?'

Megan wriggled up straighter, her attention well and truly caught. 'Can I choose?'

'Sure.'

'OK.' She nodded, and held out her arms, and Jack watched with a lump in his throat as Sal scooped the youngster up, kissed her cheek and settled down on the chair as if she was going to read a story.

'Right, now, while Jack does that, why don't you tell me how you did it, because I bet it was really exciting.'

'I was running away,' she said, 'and Toby chased me, and then I tripped up and hit my head on the door.'

'Oh. What colour is it?'

'What?'

'The door.'

'Um—white,' she said, sounding puzzled. Jack could understand that. He was puzzled, too, but it was keeping Megan still and focussed while he got the hair out of the way, so he didn't care.

All became clear, though, when Sally sucked in her breath and said in a conspiratorial tone, 'Ooh. Did you bleed on it?'

'Yes—lots—and the carpet.'

'Oh, dear. My son Alex got a bump on the nose from his little brother and he bled all over the carpet, too.'

Jack remembered it well. He remembered the look on Sally's face when he'd handed her the tissues. He remembered how beautiful she'd looked in the dark red dress. And he remembered the dance...

He swabbed the cut carefully, blotted it dry, laid the strands of hair over Sally's fingers where she was holding Megan's head firmly against that soft, pillowy chest and tried not to think about what was under her tunic.

He leant a little closer, but he couldn't see the cut clearly enough to glue it, so he dropped onto one knee and propped his other leg up with his foot flat on the floor and shifted closer. Still not close enough. He shifted again, and froze. Bad move, that. Her knee was pressed firmly against his groin, but there was nothing he could do, because he had the glue in his hand and the child was still and it was now or never...

She felt the heat flow through her body like a river.

Her knee was jammed firmly—grief, just *there*, of all places!—and she couldn't move. If it hadn't been for the intense look of concentration on his face and the muscle jumping in his jaw, she would have thought he'd set it up, but it was just one of those things.

'All done, sweetheart. Brave girl,' he said, and stroked her hair. His fingers curled around her head, and the backs of them brushed against Sally's breast, and they both jerked as if they'd been shot.

Megan slid off her lap and ran to her mother, burying her face in her mother's front again, and Sally stood up hastily and moved away, her legs burning. Jack was getting to his feet, brushing off his trousers, fussing with the gloves and sitting at the desk to write up the notes.

He didn't thank her, didn't look at her, didn't say a word to the child, so she smiled at Megan and her mother, excused herself to get the stickers and slipped out, dragging in the first lungful of air for what seemed like hours.

'Here,' she said to Megan when she returned, letting her choose which ones she wanted and pressing them firmly onto the back of her hand. 'That's really pretty,' she said, and stroked her hair out of her eyes. 'And Jack didn't get any glue in your hair. Isn't he clever?'

'He's funny,' Megan said, and Sally found a smile.

'Yes—but he knows it, so it doesn't count,' she said, and left them to it.

The waiting room was heaving, but the next few cases were slow, routine and didn't occupy her mind at all. Oh, for Resus, she thought, but she'd been rostered on cubicles. Lousy move.

Too much contact with Jack—way too much! He kept popping up like a bad penny, sticking his head round the curtain every other minute, and every time she came out of a cubicle, she could feel his eyes on her.

However long could one shift be?

She went out the front again, broke up a fight and pulled out the next set of notes. It was a drunk, with a nasty gash down his cheek from what was probably a bottle.

'Darren Wright?' she said, and turned to his companions when they shambled to their feet to follow him. 'He doesn't need an audience,' she told them firmly, and shut the door in their faces. 'Right, Darren, let's get this sorted.'

'I seen you before—last time,' he slurred.

She looked at him more closely, and nodded. 'I remember. I had to call Security. Let's not go through that again this time, eh?'

She cleaned the cut up but, of course, it stung and he started throwing his weight around and yelling, so she stopped and moved towards the curtain. 'Are you going to stop that and let me help you, or are you going down to the police station and letting the police surgeon sew you up down there?'

He subsided, more or less, and she finished her cleaning up and reached for the steristrips. 'It doesn't need stitches. I'm going to stick it together with little bits of tape,' she said, but he shook his head belligerently.

'You're only saying that so you can get rid of me quicker. I want stitches.'

'It'll scar,' she warned him.

'So?'

'And I have to give you a local anaesthetic. It stings. A lot.'

'That's OK. I'm hard.'

Right. Not that hard. The first prick of the needle had him screaming, and the curtain was whipped back out of the way just as he lunged at her.

'I don't think so,' Jack said, getting him firmly by the shoulder and pressing him back into the chair. 'Now, you heard the lady, you don't need stitches. All you need is tape, and either you sit there quietly while it's done, or we can refuse to treat you.'

'You can't refuse.'

'Watch me,' he said, folding his arms and staring the youth down.

Darren subsided, grumbling under his breath, and Jack took the steristrips out of her hand and stuck Darren's face together, gave him a tetanus shot and sent him on his way, then ripped off his gloves, muttering something about drunks, and looked at his watch.

'Come on, let's get out of here. Your shift finished ages ago.'

It had? She checked her watch and blinked in surprise. It was after half nine.

'I was coping fine, you know,' she told him conversationally, and he just arched a brow.

'Yeah, right. I could see how well you were coping. He was about to beat you to death.'

'Nonsense. He's just an idiot.'

'Idiot or not, he's trouble, and you shouldn't have to put up with it. Now, come on, let's get out of here before there's a majax or something.'

'They'd call us back,' she pointed out, but he just snorted and headed for the staffroom, ditching his stethoscope and reaching for his jacket in his locker.

'I'll walk you to your car in case Darren and his mates are still hanging about, waiting for you,' he said, and so her chance to slip away from him was gone. When they emerged from the building, however, she was grateful for his solid bulk beside her, because Darren and friends were still there, loitering about with trouble on their minds.

Just then a police car rolled up and two officers that she recognised got out.

'Move them on, John,' she murmured to the older one. 'We've stuck young Darren's face up, but they're still hanging around. Maybe waiting for whoever had a go at him to turn up.'

'Most likely. Don't worry, I'll sort them out. I've got a feeling they're just the lads we're looking for. 'Night, Sally.'

''Night, John.' She turned to Jack and forced a smile. 'I'll be fine now, you can head on home.'

'I was going to ask you to drop me off at the takeaway,' he said. 'Unless you want to join me?'

'At Annie and Patrick's?' she said doubtfully.

He shrugged. 'Or we could go somewhere.'

Somewhere loud and bright and busy, without a glimmer of romance.

She wasn't hugely hungry, even though she'd missed lunch and the sandwich had been all she'd had since breakfast, but the thought was tempting. Too tempting. 'There's an Italian,' she suggested, without allowing herself to think about it too much, and he nodded.

'Sounds good.'

But it was heaving when they pulled up outside, and the next place they tried was the same.

'Oh, give up. I'll eat toast,' he said.

She hesitated, not ready to give up and not looking too closely at the reasons. 'I could make you some pasta with pesto,' she offered slowly, and he went very still.

His eyes glittered in the darkness, searching her face, and she could hear her heart beating while she waited for his answer.

'You know what'll happen if I come back.'

She swallowed hard, and nodded. 'Yes,' she said, but she was answering quite a different question, and he knew it.

His breath hissed in sharply, and he turned away, then his voice came softly to her in the velvet dark.

'Are you sure?'

'Yes,' she said again, and with fingers that weren't quite steady she put the car into gear and headed towards home.

Jack tried to breathe deeply, slowing his heart rate, repeating the word 'calm' to himself over and over again.

It didn't work. Nothing worked. Not after touching her today, first bumping into her leg as they'd sat down, then having to kneel with her shin pressed against him so intimately that she must, just *must* have known how he felt, then the backs of his fingers brushing against her breast as he'd stroked the child's head.

Each touch had set off a wildfire, and they were running together now, burning him up. It was going to take more than a little mantra to calm him down. A damn great slug of ketamine might do it—enough to fell a horse.

She turned into her drive, pulled up by the front door and cut the engine.

'Coming?' she said, and he nearly choked.

Nothing had changed.

Well, that was rubbish. Loads had changed, but not the way she felt when he touched her, the way he seemed to know just where and how to do it, to take her to the brink again and again and again before finally driving her over it in glorious, spectacular freefall.

She turned her head and caught him studying her, his face serious. 'What is it?' she asked, suddenly aware of her nakedness and curiously shy.

'You're beautiful,' he said, his voice gruff. His hand reached out and stroked slowly down over her skin, flirting with her breasts, teasing her nipples to attention before moving on, lying flat and warm and firm against her abdomen, his long fingers splayed out over the soft curve left by childbirth.

Well, childbirth and too much chocolate. She sucked it in, and he shook his head and leant over, brushing his lips against the skin in a tender gesture that made her swallow suddenly.

'Beautiful. One hundred per cent pure woman.'

'I could do with losing weight.'

'Who says? I think you're gorgeous.'

'You're biased.'

'That's fine. I'm the one who's with you.'

He lay down again, drawing her into his arms and kissing her lips with the same tenderness. 'I've missed you, Sal,' he said, and the unexpectedness of it, the sincerity in his voice, brought tears to her eyes. It was almost as if he was saying *I love you,* but he wasn't, and she needed to remember that. Needed to remember all sorts of things.

She touched his face. 'Oh, Jack—I've missed you, too, but there are so many things...'

Guilt swamped her, guilt and uncertainty and—

His kiss stole her breath. 'There's nothing we can't work through,' he said softly. 'It's been too long. We should have been together all this time. Maybe now we can find a way.'

She closed her eyes. How? Never mind anything else, there was still Clare in the background, and Chloe. How could she ask him to leave his wife and daughter for her? He hadn't been prepared to ten years ago, why should he now? And if he did, should she trust him?

Besides, this was about so much more than just her.

'Hungry?'

Hungry? Absolutely not, but she'd promised him food and they hadn't even made it up the stairs the first time. They'd hardly made it to her bed in her new room the second. And it was nearly midnight now.

'What do you fancy?'

He smiled slowly and threw back the quilt. 'Well, apart from you, lightly brushed with oil and served warm on a bed of, well, any bed, really, I'm sure we can find something.'

She turned away from the wicked twinkle in his eyes

and stood up, putting on her dressing-gown to cover a body she was still not sure of. 'I've got fresh pasta in the fridge, and pesto, and salads and peppers and things. There might be some ham, too.'

'Sounds good.' He pulled on his snug jersey shorts and held out his hand, and she slid hers into it. Their fingers threaded together, and he drew her closer, feathered a kiss over her forehead and led her downstairs.

She put the kettle on, poured the boiling water into the pan and turned round with the pasta in her hand to find him watching her with dark, hungry eyes.

'How long does that take to cook?'

'About three minutes. It's fresh, not dried.'

'Not long enough,' he said. Taking it from her and throwing it aside, he lifted her easily and put her on the edge of the worktop.

'Jack, what on earth are you doing?' she asked on a bubble of laughter that turned instantly to need as he untied her dressing-gown and slid his hot, firm hands down over her body, parting her thighs and easing her closer.

'Isn't it obvious? I'm keeping the cook happy,' he murmured, and she gasped as he slid home, his eyes glittering. 'How on earth have I lived without you?' he groaned, and, anchoring her hips with his hands, he drove into her, taking her higher and higher with every stroke.

'Jack!' she screamed, her hands locking on his shoulders, her body convulsing around his as he gave one final thrust and shuddered against her, his head falling to her shoulder. She could feel his heartbeat through his ribs, hear hers drowning out everything, including common sense, and she rested her head against his and let her body come slowly back down to earth.

A long moment later, he stirred, lifting his head and giving her a lazy, self-satisfied grin. 'Now you can cook the pasta,' he murmured.

She laughed and slapped his shoulder, her fingers curling lightly over the warm, damp skin, sliding up to cup his neck and draw him back to her for a kiss. 'Don't push your luck, I might poison you,' she advised, and slid down to the floor, gathered her dressing-gown around her and turned her attention back to the food, a self-satisfied smile that she could do nothing about playing around her lips.

'Where the hell were you last night?'

He laughed wryly. 'I haven't been asked that since I was about sixteen,' he retorted, and walked into the kitchen, Patrick hard on his heels. 'Hiya, Tuppence, how you doing? Morning, Annie.'

She looked up from the dishwasher, her eyes searching, her face serious. 'Katie, darling, why don't you go and find your trainers and make sure you've got some good thick socks on ready to go. You've got ten minutes.'

Katie smiled up at him as she flitted past, and he rumpled her hair and grinned and then took a deep breath, ready for the firing squad.

Not a moment too soon.

Patrick got off the first shot. 'You told me—'

'I know,' he said softly. He could still hear his own words echoing in the room. *What the hell do you take me for? The poor bloody woman's marriage has just fallen apart!*

'But?'

'But I love her, and I think she loves me, and we should have been together for the last nine, nearly ten years.'

'Did you ask her if she loves you?'

'No—neither did I tell her that I love her, not that it's any of your business. I was taking your advice—giving her time.'

Patrick snorted. 'You're supposed to do the whole I-love-you thing before you spend the night with her,' he growled softly.

Annie paused, her hands full of cups, and gave him an odd look. 'You had an affair before, didn't you?' she asked, and he laughed humourlessly.

'Oh, yes. I thought—but then Clare came along and scuppered everything.'

'But you were working together, weren't you? Didn't that make it really difficult afterwards?'

He shook his head. 'Not because of that, no, because it was the end of my rotation. I started my next job in another hospital at the beginning of August, and Clare rolled up right at the end of July.'

'July?' Annie looked at him intently for a moment, then turned back to the dishwasher. 'Um—do you know if Sally's made a picnic?'

He gave a short cough of laughter. 'Ah—the picnic wasn't exactly high on our list of conversation topics, but you know Sally. If she said she was going to do it, she will have done it. And she put something in the car just before we left. I didn't see what was in it, but it was a small rucksack. I didn't pay much attention to it, to be honest.' Too busy looking at her, at the soft light in her eyes, the tender smile she'd been giving him...

'If you hurt her—'

'What?' He turned to face Patrick angrily. 'I love her, dammit. I've waited nearly ten years for a chance to tell her that again. I'm not going to hurt her now, am I?' And he pushed past him, ran upstairs and changed into jeans and a clean shirt.

He was just zipping up the jeans when Katie appeared in the doorway. 'Patrick's only cross with you because you didn't tell him where you were going to be. I expect he was worried. Mummy gets like that with me if I'm not where I say I'll be.'

He looked up from shoving his feet into trainers and grinned at her. 'It's OK, squirt. I can handle Patrick. You all set?'

She nodded, and he followed her downstairs to find the others. They were in the kitchen, deep in conversation, and they stopped abruptly when he went in. Annie couldn't meet his eye, and Patrick looked ready to kill.

So not over yet, then, he thought, and sighed inwardly. Maybe it was time to find somewhere else to live for a while.

'All ready?' Patrick asked Katie, and she nodded. Then he turned to Jack, his eyes almost hostile. 'Are you still coming?'

'Do you have a problem with that?'

Annie went still, and Patrick shrugged. 'Just…'

He arched a brow. 'Just?'

'You know…'

Jack laughed shortly and turned on his heel. 'I'll follow you in my car,' he said abruptly, and went out through the front door, leaving them to close it.

Jack wasn't with them.

Sally had been hovering near the car park, waiting for them, not knowing if she wanted him there or not, but when they drew up without him, she felt a ridiculous sense of let-down.

And then his car turned in behind theirs and her heart lifted. She had to stop herself from running over to him, and made herself wait until he got out and wandered towards her with a wry smile.

'We're in the doo-doo,' he said softly.

Oh, lord. She felt the heat climb her cheeks and turned away a little. 'What did they say?'

'Annie? Nothing much—asked a few questions about our affair years ago. Patrick, on the other hand, played the heavy father with me.'

She laughed quietly. 'Oh, I can imagine that. Bless him. He's such a sweetheart.'

Jack snorted and looked around, thoroughly unconvinced at that. 'This is a charity thing, isn't it?'

'Yes—you pay to join in. Well, the adults do.'

'Have you paid yet?'

She shook her head. 'Not yet.'

'I'll do it for you. What about the Corrigans? Have they got advance tickets or anything?'

She shook her head again. 'It's all pay on the day.'

'I'll get theirs, too, then.'

He wandered off towards the marshall, and Annie came over to her. Katie had run off to join the other children, Patrick was peering at one of his tyres—probably quite unnecessarily, she thought—and that left them alone together. How convenient.

Annie gave her a searching look and smiled tentatively. 'You OK?'

'Don't give me a hard time,' Sally warned.

Annie looked stricken, and shook her head slowly. 'Do you know what you're doing?'

'Not really. It's probably the stupidest thing I've done

in years. But—I love him, Annie. I know it's crazy. I know it can't last—'

'Mum, look, I've found a wood louse.'

'Lovely. Put it back, darling,' she said automatically. 'We'll be going soon.'

Ben darted off to return the bug to its habitat, and Sally looked around her, finding Alex deep in conversation with Jack. Her heart skittered, but he just grinned at the boy and came back to her, brandishing tickets at Annie.

'Here—I paid for yours while I was there.'

Her smile was wary. 'Is that a peace offering? If so, you probably need to give them to Patrick.'

He gave a grunt of laughter and handed them to her. 'Just take them, Annie. Patrick can sort himself out. He's not my problem, and neither will I be his soon.'

Because he was moving on. How silly of her to have forgotten it, even for last night, but by the time he'd finished with her she hadn't remembered her own name, never mind all the hundred and one vital reasons why it had been such a lousy idea.

'Please, go and talk to him,' Annie begged, and with a sigh he took the tickets back and went over to Patrick's car.

Sally looked around for the children. It was time to start heading off on the ten-mile trail around the nature reserves and woodland, and back through the park. It was the walk they'd done in October, when Patrick and Annie had first met, and she knew it would have sentimental connotations for them.

She turned to Annie and found a smile.

'Go and walk with Patrick. We'll keep an eye on Katie for you. And mind you don't get blisters!'

'I never get blisters now, not with your boots, and

Patrick can wait a minute for me. I'm worried about you, Sally.'

'Well, don't be. I'll be fine. We all will.' Somehow, although she wasn't thinking about what would happen when he went back to Clare and Chloe. It was too hideous to contemplate.

'Just remember—we're here for you if you need us. We're your friends.'

'I thought Patrick was Jack's friend?'

She sighed. 'He is, but—they had words this morning.'

'Jack said. I'm sorry, I don't want to drag you two into this. It's all ancient history.'

'Not that ancient—not any more, is it? And Patrick's very protective of you. He was just worried you'd be hurt.'

She laughed softly and hugged Annie hard, the emotion welling in her chest. 'Thank you, but he doesn't need to fight Jack over this. We can sort it out between us.'

'In other words, butt out?'

She smiled. 'In the nicest way.'

Annie chewed her lip, as if she wanted to say something else, but Alex and Katie came running up and she just shook her head and turned round, waiting for Patrick to catch her up.

'Come on, kids, off we go,' Sally said, and walked on, Ben at her side bouncing along sideways and chattering at her about woodlice and earwigs and other creepy-crawlies while Alex and Katie led the way. And then Jack was there, too, grinning at Ben.

'You OK, sport?'

'Yeah, I'm fine. Do you like bugs?'

He chuckled. 'Probably more than your mother.'

'She hates bugs,' Ben said, and opened his hand.

Another unfortunate creature, Sally thought, and glanced at Alex and Katie. They were still just ahead, chattering like starlings, full of energy.

Good, she thought. He's safely occupied. But then Fliss came over, and Ben ran off to see one of her children, and Jack and Tom ended up walking together for a while, deep in conversation.

And the next time she looked, he was with Alex, kicking a football backwards and forwards between them, teaching him to dribble.

She heard Alex laugh, and Jack was pulling a face and chasing after the ball, and then Alex ran back to her, eyes alight.

'Mummy, can Jack come over to our house some time and teach me football? He's really cool and he says he can teach me all sorts of things—did you know he'd done bungee jumping and white-water rafting and stuff? He's amazing. Can he come? Please?'

She felt the panic building and wondered what on earth had made her think she could deal with this. It wasn't going to go away, even if Jack did.

'Maybe. I'll ask your father.'

Oh, God.

'Cool.' And he ran off, back to his new idol, and Sally stopped in her tracks and watched them together. They were laughing at each other, sharing a joke, heads thrown back, eyes crinkled, and as Patrick and Annie came up alongside her, they followed her eyes and stopped walking.

'Oh, my God,' Annie whispered. 'Sally—does he know?'

She shook her head, her heart pounding, nausea rising in her throat.

But just then he looked up, his smile fading, and caught

them all staring at him, their eyes going from him to Alex and back again.

He tipped his head on one side in a quizzical gesture, and Alex copied it. 'What's wrong, Mum?'

She opened her mouth to speak, but no words would come out. There were no words—or, at least, none that would make it any better or any different.

Then Jack glanced down at Alex, then back to them, and she saw realisation dawn.

He sucked in a breath, turned on his heel and strode briskly off, leaving Alex standing in the middle of the path, his face puzzled. 'Jack? Wait for me.'

'Alex, leave him. He just wants some time to himself,' Sally said hurriedly, but then Jack stopped and slowly turned and walked back to Alex, his eyes on Sally.

'It's OK. I think actually I've had quite enough time by myself.'

She swallowed and forced herself to meet his eyes. They were blazing with anger, and something else—something that could have been pride.

Their football skidded across the path and he lifted a foot and trapped it against the ground. He looked down at Alex and his face twisted for a second.

'Come on, then, son,' he said clearly, rumpling his hair, 'let's find out what you're made of.'

And then he smiled and kicked the ball towards him.

CHAPTER EIGHT

'WE NEED to talk.'

Jack's eyes sliced through Sally. 'Oh, do we ever. But not here. Not now.'

She looked round at them all, grouped under the trees, eating their picnic, Patrick and Annie carefully avoiding looking at them, the children oblivious and full of energy.

He was right. It wasn't the place, but it was certainly time.

'Later, then,' she suggested, dreading it and yet feeling in a way a sense of relief that at last it was out. 'When the boys have gone to bed.'

'Not while they're in the house.'

'Why?' she asked with gentle cynicism. 'Because you can't yell at me then?'

'I don't want to yell at you,' he said tightly. 'I just want answers—nine years' worth. And I intend to have them, but not when my son might overhear. I'm not that crazy—quite.'

She nodded and looked away, unable to take the anger and resentment in his eyes. He might not want to yell at her, but he looked as if he could quite easily knock down the nearest tree just by glaring at it.

He screwed up his sandwich wrapper and jackknifed up off the ground in one fluid movement, the coiled energy radiating off him in waves. Alex broke off in the middle of his sentence and scrambled to his feet. 'Are we going?'

Jack's face softened, and he smiled at Alex and shook his head. 'Not yet. I'm just going to have a chat to Tom. You stay here with Katie and your brother.'

'But can I walk with you when we go?'

Something flickered across Jack's face that could have been pain, and he nodded. 'Sure,' he said softly, and with a twisted smile he walked away. Alex dropped back down onto the rug and picked up an apple, crunching on it while he watched Jack with one eye.

She closed her eyes to hold back the tears. She'd have to talk to David—tell him that Jack knew. And between them they'd have to work out how to tell Alex, because there was no way Jack was going away quietly. Not now.

And having seen him with Alex, seen the look of pride and wonder on his face, she wouldn't contemplate asking him to. He had the right to get to know his son, and Alex had a right to know his father.

'Are you OK?'

She opened her eyes and looked at Annie. She'd shifted closer, so she was sitting right beside her now, arms wrapped round her slender knees, her face worried. Sally found a smile from somewhere.

'Yes,' she said a little unevenly. 'I'm fine.'

'You're a lousy liar.'

Her smile wobbled and she shook her head. 'Don't— not here. Annie, he wants to talk. Tonight.'

'Do you want me to have the boys?'

She shook her head. 'No. I'll ask David—invent some excuse about a changed shift or something to tell them.'

'Unless we take the boys straight away after the walk

to give you time to talk this afternoon? I could give them supper.'

'But you're feeling rough.'

'I'll be fine. Patrick can cook.'

'Are you sure?'

Annie slipped her arm round Sally's shoulders and hugged her hard. 'Of course I'm sure. It'll be fun for them and, let's face it, they won't be any trouble, not after such a long walk. Anyway, you and Jack need to talk.'

She felt her throat close with dread. 'You're right. Thanks, Annie. I'm sorry I didn't tell you, but—'

'That's OK. I understand.' Annie stood up and started clearing away the debris of the picnic, and Sally looked at her boys and wondered how they'd take this latest bit of news to rock their boat. Oh, lord, how much more?

She stood up and brushed off her knees, then looked up to see Jack still talking to Tom. Talking to him, but watching her.

And they still had about three more miles to walk.

'Tea?'

Jack made a rude sound and followed her into the kitchen. 'No, I don't want tea, dammit. I don't want to be civilised and polite. You're lucky I'm not a violent man, because right now I could strangle you with my bare hands.'

She swallowed and turned away from him, fiddling with the kettle for something to do. She got mugs out, teabags, milk…

'Are you going to talk to me or are you going to do that anyway?' he growled.

'Of course I'm going to talk to you, but I need tea.'

'And I need to know why it's taken over nine years to find out I've got a child!'

He slammed his fist down on the worktop next to her, making the mugs rattle, and she froze.

He was so angry, and what did she really know about him? He was a good doctor, an amazing lover, he had an outrageous sense of humour and his diet was appalling, but apart from that and the wanderlust, she knew nothing. What if he was violent? OK, he'd said he wasn't and he'd never been anything but gentle with her physically, but what if he really was…?

'I'm sorry,' he said, moving away from her, ramming his hands through his hair and turning towards her with anguished eyes. 'It's just—to know that I have a child, that for nine years Alex has been growing up without me—why didn't you tell me, Sal? How could you have kept that from me for *nearly ten years*? You should have told me!'

The injustice of that stung her, and she stood her ground. 'What was I supposed to do, Jack? You were married to Clare! She was having your child. Did you really expect me to come after you and say, "Oh, by the way, Clare's not the only woman having your child but, hey, that's cool, you can have access whenever you want"? And anyway, by the time I realised it was morning sickness and not just stress, you'd gone.'

'So you did the next best thing and married the first sucker to come along. Poor bastard. Does he think Alex is his child?'

She wrapped her arms round her waist and hugged herself. 'No. Of course he doesn't. He knew I was pregnant when he married me. It was only a few weeks before Alex was born. It was never a secret.'

'And does he know that Alex is mine and not just some random stranger's?'

She nodded. 'He does now. He realised at the wedding—when we were dancing. But he didn't know your name. I never told him.' Mostly because even to think it, never mind speak it, had simply reopened the wound.

'He must be some kind of a saint, marrying a woman pregnant with another man's child.'

She bit her lip and turned back to the kettle. 'I'm making tea. You can join me if you want.'

'Oh, for God's sake, give me tea, then, if it makes you happy.'

'I don't care one way or the other. And David isn't a saint. He's just a good, decent man, and he was lonely, and so was I, and his wife had died and—well, it just seemed to be the sensible thing to do. And he's been a good father—an excellent father—and I won't hear a word against him. He's been wonderful with Alex, and he couldn't have loved him any more if he'd been his own. He's brought him up really well.'

'I can see that, and when I'm feeling rational, no doubt I'll be grateful, but Alex is mine, and I should have been doing it.'

'Except you were bringing up Chloe.'

He snorted and turned away, resting against the door-frame and staring down the garden, his face shielded from her so she couldn't see his expression when he said, 'So why didn't you tell me? I mean then, OK, I can see it was difficult. I still think you were wrong not to tell me, but now? What about now? Surely you could have found some time in the past two and a half weeks to tell me. I mean, for heaven's sake, we've seen enough of each other—or were you never going to tell me?'

She fished the teabags out and plopped them in the sink, then added milk. 'I don't know.'

He jerked away from the wall and spun round to face her. 'What do you mean, you don't know? How can you not know? He's my *son*, dammit! I have a right to know—and so does he!'

'Why?' she asked flatly. 'So you can go back to your wife and child and leave his life in even more chaos? I can't let you do that to him. He's gone through enough.'

But his eyes were puzzled, his brows drawn together in a frown. 'I'm not going anywhere. I'm not with Clare anymore.'

She snorted. 'I've heard that one before. Forgive me if I don't believe it.'

'Oh, you can believe it. Clare and I are well and truly over—I thought you realised that.'

'You've left her?'

'No—she left me, about seven years ago. For Chloe's father. They've been married for almost seven years.'

It took a moment for that to sink in, and then her tea slopped and splashed down her jeans, dribbling onto her feet. She put it down.

'So—Chloe's not yours? After all that?' she whispered, and he shook his head.

He didn't have a child. All those years she'd pictured him with Clare and their children, and Chloe hadn't even been his. He need never have left, need never have married her and gone, could have been with Alex all this time.

'Ironic, isn't it?' he said with a bitter little laugh. 'She wasn't pregnant with my child, and I married her, and yet all along you were.'

She shook her head. 'Not all along. It must have been

that last night. That was the other reason I couldn't come after you and tell you, because I begged you to make love to me. It wasn't as if it was your fault, and I didn't feel I could ruin your chance of happiness with Clare because of something stupid I'd done. I knew you wouldn't refuse me. Knew you couldn't, and I had to touch you one last time, even though I knew you belonged to Clare. So I didn't really give you a choice, and that took away my own.'

He laughed, a sad, abrupt sound that ended on what could have been a sob. 'Oh, Sal, there's always a choice. You didn't need to beg me. I thought it was the last chance I had to touch you, and I ended up giving you a child that I didn't even know about.'

He turned away, his shoulders heaving as he struggled for control, and then he drew in a steadying breath and turned back to her. 'Can I see his bedroom?'

She searched his face and found anguish and desperation and a terrible need for knowledge. She could understand that. She would have felt exactly the same.

'Of course,' she said softly, and led him upstairs, pushing open the door of Alex's room and standing back to let him go in. 'This is it.'

His son's bedroom.

He looked around, finding the typical clutter of a nine-year-old's bedroom—books, toys, puzzles, clothes kicked under the edge of the bed, but nothing electronic, he was glad to see. There was a football poster on the wall, a dog-eared teddy on the bed. He picked it up and lay down on the bed, staring at the ceiling and seeing the room from Alex's viewpoint.

His son.

He swallowed hard. All these years, since he'd discovered in the cruellest way that Chloe wasn't his daughter, he'd been coming to terms with the realisation that he would never have a child. He'd known Sal was married, because he'd tried to contact her through a friend of a friend, and he'd been told she was married with a child and a baby on the way.

So any chance of happiness with her had withered and died at that point, and from then on he'd concentrated on living life to the full, going to dangerous places and doing crazy things, because after all who was there to care if he died—and all the time, he'd had a son.

Alex.

He said the name out loud, but his voice cracked and he turned his head towards the wall, staring at the poster above his head, trying to clear his vision. He felt a tear slide down his cheek and run into his hair, and then another, but he wouldn't give way.

Not in front of Sal.

And then she touched him, her hand gentle on his arm. 'I'm so sorry.'

Her voice was ragged with regret, and he turned his head and saw tears coursing down her cheeks, and somehow it didn't matter any more if he cried because, after all, if his son wasn't worth crying over, what was?

Still holding the tattered bear in his hand, he reached for her, drew her down into his arms and wept.

'Tell me about him.'

His voice was still clogged with tears, but the first storm had passed, and she lay there in his arms and told him about her pregnancy, about Alex's birth, about his child-hood, pausing to answer his questions along the way.

'Was David there?'

'Yes,' she told him, and his arms tightened.

'Good,' he said gruffly. 'You shouldn't have been alone.'

And then, 'When did he get his first tooth? Say his first word? Take his first step?'

Later, he wanted to know other things, Alex's favour-ites—colour, food, school subject, sport...

'Football. I thought you would have worked that one out.'

He gave a rusty chuckle. 'Yeah, I pretty much had, but I wondered if there was anything else.'

'Anything fast-moving,' she said with a smile. 'He takes after you in that.'

'I'd noticed he isn't like Ben. It's not just the looks—though how I didn't see it the moment I set eyes on him I don't know, because it's just like looking in a mirror and seeing myself at the same age.'

He fell silent, then after an age he said, 'You would have told me, wouldn't you? Eventually?'

She sighed. 'I don't know. If I'd known about Clare, then, yes, of course, but I really didn't. I thought you were still married.'

'And you really thought I would have made love to you?'

'Well, you did before—and *I'm* still married,' she pointed out, but he shook his head.

'Not really. Have you filed for divorce yet?'

'Not yet. We're doing the paperwork tomorrow night, and we're going to the court to file the papers on Tuesday morning. It's pretty straightforward, David says. We aren't fighting about anything.'

He was silent for a moment, then said carefully, 'Alex's birth certificate...'

'Is blank. I didn't put David down as the father, if that's what you're asking, even though we were married by then.'

She felt the tension go out of him, as if that had been a hugely important fact he'd had to establish. For a while he said nothing, then he went on, 'What was it like? Being married to him?'

She thought about it for a moment, then said softly, 'Sad, at first. I missed you endlessly, but David was very gentle and understanding, and he's been a good husband. Even if we never lit up the night sky, we loved each other. And in spite of what you said, it wasn't a loveless marriage. We had a lot of good times.'

'You were lucky,' he said. 'Right from the beginning I knew marrying Clare was a mistake.'

She shifted, turning so she could see his face, and she lifted her hand and touched his cheek, tracing the line of the tears. 'Tell me about Chloe,' she said gently, and he closed his eyes and swallowed.

'She's lovely—a lot like Katie. I adore her. I couldn't love her any more if she was my own, but I don't see her. Her father doesn't like it, so Clare used to wangle a meeting between us once a year or so, but it upset her so much she stopped doing it. She sends me the odd DVD, though, and emails me photos occasionally, and it tears me apart.'

'Hence all the running away.'

'Hence all the running away,' he echoed softly.

She felt her eyes fill again and, leaning closer, she brushed her lips against his cheek. 'I'm so sorry.'

'It's not your fault,' he said, his voice uneven, his arms

tightening around her and hugging her tenderly. 'None of it's your fault, or mine. It's just one of those things that happens, and now we have to move on.'

She nodded, and then he echoed her thoughts.

'So where do we go from here?'

'Where do you want to go?'

'Ultimately? I want him to know I'm his father. I take it he thinks David is?'

'Yes. Well, it's never come up. Why would he think anything else? He's just a child. He doesn't know about sex, about reproduction, not to the point of passing on genes. He knows people live together and have babies, but I don't know if he knows much more than that. And his world's already been shaken on its foundations.'

Jack nodded, his sigh soft with regret. 'Do you think we'll ever be able to tell him?'

'I don't know,' she said with complete honesty. 'You need to get to know him first, and he needs to get to know you.'

'And us?' he said.

She looked up at him. 'Us?' she said. 'What about us? As far as the children are concerned, there is no us.'

'Yet,' he said, and his eyes were serious. 'But there will be.'

'Not necessarily.'

'Necessarily,' he said, his voice uncompromising now, 'because I've missed the first nine years of my son's life, and I don't intend to miss any more. So you'd better get used to having me around, Sal. I'm here for the long haul, and you might as well get used to it.'

The next few days were emotionally draining.

She gave Jack all the video footage of Alex's child-hood, and on Monday evening when David came round to sort out the divorce papers she put the boys to bed, took him into the study, shut the door and told him that Jack knew.

'Oh, sweetheart,' he said, his face creasing with concern, and he drew her into his arms and hugged her gently. 'Are you OK?'

She shook her head and sniffed, and then found herself crying all over him. When she finally ground to a halt he mopped her up, held her at arm's length and studied her face, and sighed softly. 'We'll have to tell Alex some time,' he said, and she nodded.

'Not yet, though. I want to know that Jack's serious. He says he's here to stay, and he and Clare aren't married any more, which I didn't know, so maybe he means it, but before we do anything to upset Alex I want time.'

'Good. I agree. And if you want time alone together, just ask and we'll have the boys.'

'Why should we want time…?' she began, but he just smiled wryly and shook his head.

'I've known you a long time, and I've never seen you look the way you do now. You love him, don't you? It hasn't gone away.'

'No, it hasn't,' she admitted, 'but this is much more serious now than it ever was, because of Alex, and he's the only one I can really afford to be concerned about.'

'I agree—but the offer still stands. And if Jack feels the same way you do, then you really need to explore this relationship, because to have the two of you together would be the best thing for Alex in the long run, so give it a chance. For you, as well as for the boy. You're a wonderful woman, and I'd love to see you happy.'

His words touched her deeply, and she nearly started to cry again, but she dragged in a deep breath and found a smile. 'I'll keep you in touch with any developments,' she promised.

He nodded, then sat down at the desk he'd used for years and pulled out the file of important personal documents. 'Come on, we'd better sort this out—there's a lot to go through.'

They talked it all through before filling out the divorce papers—access, custody and all the legal intricacies of ending a marriage with children. By the time they'd done that, she just wanted to crawl into a corner and howl for weeks, but instead she tucked the boys up and kissed them goodnight, just feather-light kisses on their cheeks so as not to wake them, and in the morning she took them to school and met David at the court to hand in the petition.

And then, with the systematic dismantling of her life set in train, she went to work.

'Sally! Just the woman. Can you do majors for me today? I've hurt my ankle and I'd be happier on cubicles—I can hobble slowly.'

She frowned at Angie's foot and shook her head. 'Silly you—how did you do that?'

'Oh, I fell off the kerb. Stupid. Are you all right with that?'

'Sure. Have you had it looked at?'

She nodded. 'Jack's checked it for me and says it isn't broken.'

'I bet he also told you to go home and rest it,' Sally said bluntly, and Angie looked evasive. 'I knew it. Well, just don't compromise your recovery. This department's getting all too accident-prone for my liking.'

'If you're talking about Al and his hand, he's going to

be back on Monday, and Matt Jordan's back from his holiday then, too.'

'So we won't need Jack any more,' she said, feeling a surge of relief that she'd get at least the respite of work time to herself, but Angie didn't look so pleased.

'Sadly, no,' she said. 'He's a brilliant doctor. We've been so lucky to get him. It's a shame he can't stay on anyway.'

Oh, no it wasn't, she thought. There were only a few more days to go. She could cope with that, just about, but now what she craved from him was space to marshal her see-sawing emotions. Not that she'd get it yet.

'Is he on majors?' she asked, knowing before she'd finished the sentence what the answer would be. And she wouldn't have been the slightest bit surprised if he'd wangled it.

It was a long day. She felt as if she'd been through the wringer what with the weekend's revelations and going through all the divorce papers with David, writing down in black and white the arrangements for the children, but in fact that had been straightforward.

Shared custody, equal access, no hassle or wrangling, and because neither of them had an axe to grind and both of them wanted the best for the boys, it was easy.

On paper.

The practicalities would be difficult, and there would be disappointments and regrets along the line, but David was so happy, so deeply content and a totally different person now, that she couldn't wish it any other way.

And, besides, there was Jack.

Jack, and his assertion that he was there for the long

haul, and she'd better get used to it. Easier said than done. Her heart still went into overdrive every time she saw him, and she knew she'd be dead before she was used to him.

They were in one of the trolley cubicles together working on a patient with chest pain, when they heard a commotion in cubicles. She stuck her head round the corner and saw a youth running towards the exit doors, barging them open with his shoulder, and as he turned, she caught a glimpse of his face, a line of steristrips down the side.

'Darren?' she called, setting off after him, but as she drew level with the cubicles, Tom staggered out into the corridor, his eyes wide with disbelief.

'Sally? Help me,' he said, his voice a thread.

She looked down to where his hand was splayed over his shirt, a dark red stain spreading on the pale blue, and there was a blade sticking out between his fingers.

'Jack!' she yelled. 'Trolley, someone, quick!'

Angie appeared, hobbling, with a trolley. Sally rolled Tom onto it as Jack appeared and they ran for the trauma theatre.

'You're OK, mate,' Jack was saying, his Aussie accent coming through. 'We've got you. Someone get an anaesthetist down here now!'

'I'm on it,' a voice said, and Ben Maguire appeared beside them, checking Tom's pulse, yelling at him to hang on as Tom's face drained of all colour.

'Bleeding out,' he whispered, grabbing Ben's hand weakly. 'Need Theatre.'

Jack shook his head. 'No time. We've got you, Tom, just hang in there. Ben, get him under. Sal, just double-glove, we haven't got time to scrub. Get some lines into him, somebody, let's get some fluids going—and someone call the CT team! I want the thoracotomy tray now!'

She'd never seen so many people appear from nowhere. Within seconds Tom was under, intubated and Jack was opening him up, going down between his ribs, following the line of the blade down to its tip, finding the bleeding vessel with his fingers and clamping it off so that the spurting blood slowed to a fast trickle.

Jack straightened up, took a deep breath and closed his eyes. 'OK, how's his blood pressure?'

'Eighty over fifty and stable,' Ben said, his voice apparently calm.

He nodded. 'Sal, can I have some suction? And can someone get some blood for cross-match—eight units initially, please, and we'd better have two of O-neg to start. Ah, the cavalry,' he added as a surgeon came running.

'Can you let go of that?'

'Not unless you want him to die,' Jack said candidly, and the man blew out his cheeks, scrubbed and moved in to help, and within a little while all the bleeding had been arrested, the wound was closed, Tom's drain was working and he was on his way to ICU.

Jack ripped off his gloves, closed his eyes and said, 'Has anybody phoned Fliss yet?'

'I'll do it,' Sally said, realising that she was shaking all over with reaction. It was bad enough working on a stranger. A friend and a colleague was much, much tougher. She wondered how Ben was holding up. He and Tom were very close, had been for years, and he'd gone with him up to ICU.

'No, let me do it. You call Meg—she'll need some support.'

'Meg's very pregnant,' she said worriedly.

'She'll still want to know. She'll be fine, but Fliss won't.'

So she called Meg, and got her on her mobile. 'Where are you?' she asked without preamble.

'With Fliss—we're waiting for the men but they're late as usual. She's just gone to answer the phone and left me putting the kids to bed. Why?'

'Meg, go to her,' she said urgently. 'That's Jack on the phone—Tom's been stabbed. Jack operated on him and he's stable—he's gone up to ICU, but she needs to be here. It was a close call. And Ben's with him.'

'Oh, dear God,' Meg whispered. 'Don't worry, I'll bring her. I'll see you later.'

Sally put the phone down, her hands shaking violently, and Jack's arm came round her shoulders and drew her up against him. 'OK?'

'No.'

'Me neither. Let's let someone else clear up this mess and go and see him and then we'll have a coffee. That was too close for comfort.'

'I think we need to change,' she said, eyeing their blood-splattered clothes, and he gave a tiny, humourless laugh.

'You might be right.' He dragged off his scrub top, took another from the pile in the corner and pulled it on over his head, then threw her one. For once she didn't even notice his body or care about her own. Fear was good like that.

They went up to ICU, and found Ben standing by Tom's bed, arms folded, glaring at the monitor as if defying it to falter.

'We've called Fliss and Meg, they're coming,' she told him, and he nodded.

'Thanks.'

'How is he?'

'Hanging on. I can't say any more than that.'

'Any idea who did it?' Jack asked.

'I know exactly,' Sally said, and looked up at him. 'Darren Wright—our friend with the slash on his face from the other day. Saturday night.' The night they'd gone back to her house and made love all night...

Jack frowned. 'I thought the police were picking him up.'

She shrugged. 'Maybe they didn't have enough to make it stick.'

'Well, they have this time,' Ben said. 'Angie's talking to them now, showing them where it happened, and the nurse who was with him saw it all. Apparently he was looking for you two.'

Jack's frown deepened to a scowl, and with a muttered curse he dragged her into his arms. 'Bastard,' he growled, and pressed his lips against her head.

She knew what he was thinking. She was thinking it, too.

If Darren had found them, it might have been Jack lying there, not Tom—and he might not have been so lucky...

CHAPTER NINE

THEY didn't speak again.

Not to each other, at least, but the realisation that either of them could have been the victims didn't leave their minds. Sally couldn't think about anything else, and every time she looked up, Jack was looking at her with his mouth taut.

They went back down to the department, changed into their street clothes and went to talk to the police who were waiting. When they finally let them go, they headed for her car in silence, and she drove home, let them in and led him straight up to her bedroom.

Wordlessly he reached for her, taking off her clothes with shaking fingers, running his hands over her ribcage as if to check that she was, indeed, unmarked.

She knew just what he was doing. She was doing it, too, picturing Tom's chest held wide open by the spreaders, his blood pumping out all over the floor while Jack searched frantically for the leak. It could have been Jack's blood, his ribs, his body torn apart in a frenzied attempt to save life—an attempt that, thank God, had succeeded.

And they were still alive. Still breathing, their hearts

pounding, hands stroking now, reverently smoothing skin that had miraculously escaped the blade.

He carried her down onto the bed and kissed her, his lips trembling. His whole body was shaking, like hers, and he eased over her, hesitating for a moment, eyes locked with hers until he entered her with a ragged groan.

It was the only sound he made until he climaxed, his body arching over hers, a tortured sob wrenched from him as her body tightened around him, and she screamed and bit his shoulder, the scream turning into sobs as the tension freed.

He rolled to his side, taking her with him, cradling her against his heart. Still without a word, they fell asleep, waking again in the night to make love once more in silent desperation.

Then finally he drew her into his arms and held her close, and said softly, 'I could have lost you.' His voice was choked with tears.

'I know. I could have lost you, too.'

His mouth found hers, stopping the words, kissing her tenderly before drawing her head down against his shoulder and covering them with the quilt, but she couldn't sleep.

'Ring the hospital,' she said, and he sat up and used the bedside phone, ending the call after a short conversation.

'No change. He's still stable but critical. Fliss is with him.'

'Poor Fliss.'

'He's alive, Sal. Right now, that's all that matters.'

He snuggled her back against his chest, pressed his lips to her hair and stroked her shoulder rhythmically until she fell asleep again, waking only when her alarm went off at six.

He was already up, and he'd phoned the hospital again.

'Still no change,' he reported.

'Do you need to go back to Patrick and Annie's?' she asked him, and he shook his head.

'No. If I can just shower and shave here, I've got a clean shirt at work. That'll do. I'll ring them, tell them what's happened to Tom. Let's just get back to the hospital and see him.'

Tom looked awful.

Pale, unconscious, a mass of trailing tubes and wires, the machines bleeping and flashing, the hiss of the ventilator and the hum of the equipment the only sounds to break the silence.

But his heartbeat was steady, his blood pressure was good and he was still with them.

Fliss was at his side, her face drawn and her eyes only leaving his face for an instant to acknowledge their arrival. After reassuring themselves that he was still holding up, they went down to a subdued and unusually quiet department and carried on with life.

It was hard, but Sally made herself concentrate, and within a very short while she was only too glad.

A woman in her thirties was brought in and rushed to Resus, her young son with her, and Jack took her through while Sally held the boy back. The paramedic had shaken his head, and she knew it was bad news, but the boy was beside himself.

'She's not dead,' he was saying. 'She's not! I know she's not! She's just sleeping. Why won't you listen? I shouldn't have rung you!'

It was something they heard all the time, grieving relatives unable to believe the terrible reality, but after a moment she realised that there was something different about this little one. A deep conviction, an absolute certainty.

And…sleeping? 'Sweetheart, has this ever happened before?' she asked, a suspicion forming at the back of her mind, and he nodded.

'She's got cat-something.'

'Cataplexy?'

He nodded, and Sally held his hand and opened the door of Resus.

'Her son says she has cataplexy,' she told Jack, and he turned to look at her, then the boy.

'Put her on that monitor—see if there's any heart activity,' he snapped, and seconds later it was there, a faint trace, just a slow, slightly irregular and very weak heartbeat.

'She can hear you,' the boy said. 'She just can't answer. She'll be scared, 'cos everyone said she was dead, and she's not.'

'Well, you'd better come and talk to her, then, hadn't you?' Jack said, lifting him up and holding him so he could kiss her face and touch her.

'Hiya, Mummy,' he said worriedly, his little voice wobbling. 'It's OK, they know now. You're all right. I'm here.'

'There,' Jack said, putting him down and ruffling his hair gently. 'She'll be feeling much better now. Thanks for helping us. Can you go and wait with Sally? Maybe she'll find you a drink and something to eat, and we'll get the doctor in charge of this kind of thing down to see her, OK? And you can come back in a minute.'

Jack found them a short while later, took the boy back to see his mother, who'd now woken, and then stuck his head round the plaster-room door. Sally was just clearing up after taking a cast off a fractious toddler, and she smiled at him.

'OK now?'

'Yes—thanks to you.'

'Well, thanks to her son, really. You hear such dreadful stories of people with cataplexy being taken to the mortuary because nobody's put them on a monitor.'

He grinned. 'If it's any consolation, we were about to do that. There's no danger she would have been carted off on my watch, but her GCS was incredibly low. She was utterly unresponsive, no pupil reaction, nothing. I got told off for pinching her too hard when she came to, and he's absolutely right, she did know everything that was going on.'

'Good job you weren't chatting up the nurses, then,' she teased, and he just grinned again.

'How do you know I wasn't?'

'Were you?'

His eyes sobered and he shook his head. 'No. I wasn't. There's only one nurse I'm interested in chatting up, and I think she knows who she is.'

Sally felt her cheeks warm and she looked away. 'Any news of Tom?'

'Same. It could be days.'

'Poor Fliss. She looked dreadful. I'll go and sit with her in my lunch-break, see if I can make her eat before she fades away.'

She wouldn't eat, but she gripped Sally's hand and seemed grateful for her presence, and after half an hour Sally hugged her and left to go back down to the department, wondering why she was walking around and Tom was lying there. Darren had been her patient, and it was so unjust that it should have been Tom...

'You OK?'

'It should have been me,' she said woodenly, and Jack took her into the staffroom and gave her a coffee and the remains of his sandwich.

'It shouldn't have been anyone,' he corrected her. 'The man's mad. They've got him, though. I've just heard they picked him up in the night and charged him with attempted murder.'

So he was safely out of the way. Finally, Sally found she could relax at work and stop looking over her shoulder. Almost.

And at home she was too busy to think about it. Because Fliss didn't move from Tom's bedside, his parents took it in turns to look after the children and keep her company, and Sally did her share, having Michael and Abby for the night on Wednesday and Thursday as Fliss had done for her boys so many times before.

The babies stayed at home, and Catherine and Andrew helped their grandparents, but during that initial period it was hell for all of them.

And Jack was brilliant.

He did much of the fetching and carrying of the children, spending the evenings with her to take the catering off her hands, and making it all more normal, somehow. And he didn't once mention Alex. He just got on with it, showing her another side of him she hadn't known he had, and at the end of the week, when Tom was out of ICU and it all looked much better, instead of taking the easy way out, he moved over to Fliss and Tom's house, into their little flat over the kitchen, and carried on helping Fliss with her children.

And, of course, he took over Tom's role in the depart-

ment in Matt Jordan's absence, which meant that getting
to know his son went onto the back burner, but he didn't
even mention it to Sally, and her respect for him soared.

Then Fliss popped in on Saturday to report on Tom's
progress just as Sally was getting to the end of her shift,
and asked her over for supper.

'I can't,' she said regretfully. 'David and Wendy are
away tonight—they're going to a play and staying over in
a hotel—and I said I'd have the boys and Harriet.'

'So bring them. I'm sure Abby and Michael would be
delighted to have company their own age, and Abby certainly would be thrilled to have a girl to balance the
books a bit.'

'But you'll be visiting Tom,' she said, not wanting to
take that away from her, but she shook her head.

'His parents are doing it tonight and, anyway, he's exhausted, he's had so many visitors. They let the kids in
today, so tonight will be brief and quiet. I'll pop in later to
say goodnight, but you're more than welcome. In fact,
why don't you stay over? The pool's up and running, and
tomorrow's supposed to be a scorcher for May.'

It sounded as if Fliss really wanted her there, and maybe
she did, for moral support. And why not go? She wasn't
working on Sunday, there was nothing to prevent it, and,
knowing Jack was there, and how much he wanted to see
Alex, she agreed. At last, with the tension about Tom's con-
dition finally easing, maybe their attention could switch
back to his relationship with his son.

'Thanks—we will,' she said, hugging Fliss and noticing
how thin she'd got over the last few days. 'I'd better clear
it with Wendy first, though, but I'm sure it'll be fine. And
I'll make sure you eat,' she added, and Fliss laughed.

'Oh, I had lunch today. Tom was so much better, and suddenly I realised I was starving. I don't think I've eaten since Tuesday lunchtime.'

'Idiot,' she said affectionately. 'I'll go and fetch the children and come over now.'

It was another chaotic evening, with the four lively youngsters being joined by Harriet, and after a noisy and rather boisterous supper Jack found himself being pressed into service again as football coach to the three boys while the girls went into the tree-house Tom had built and giggled a lot.

The two youngest, not more than babies really, had been carted off by Fliss to be bathed and put to bed, Catherine, the oldest, was out with friends, Andrew was upstairs on the internet and that left Sally, sitting on the terrace with a glass of wine, watching Jack.

So he did what any red-blooded male would do, and showed off his skills.

Badly.

The header came straight in her direction, knocked the wine all down her front and left her soaked and spluttering.

'I'm sorry!' he yelled, running over and looking down at her, but her T-shirt was soaked, her eyes were filled with laughter and he suddenly realised it had been a week since he'd made love to her.

A week that had changed his life.

'Are you OK, Mum?' Alex asked, running up to her and staring at her in horrified fascination. 'Oops. She'll kill you,' he said, tipping his head back and looking up at Jack with a mischievous twinkle he recognised only too well.

He swallowed the lump in his throat, ruffled his son's hair and retrieved the ball.

'I think I'll probably get away with it. Have to do a lot of grovelling, though.'

'Grovelling doesn't work,' Alex said. 'She gets cross if you grovel. She says you have to face the music.'

Jack pulled a doubtful face. 'Oh, dear. Sounds serious.'

But Alex laughed. 'Nah. She'll just give you jobs to do. I expect you'll have to wash the car.'

'Forfeits, eh? I like forfeits,' he said, and Sally bit her lip to trap the laughter he could see in her eyes.

He grinned, dropped the football on his foot and bounced it in the air a few times, winked and headed it back to the boys on the lawn, then followed, leaving her to blot up the wine because, frankly, if he'd touched her, he would have made an utter fool of himself.

'What happened to your T-shirt?'

Sally pulled a wry face and nodded towards the football team. 'It seems the coach isn't as good as he thought.'

Fliss chuckled, then tipped her head on one side and gave Sally a searching look. 'Tom told me you used to know each other years ago.'

She looked at Fliss and wondered how long it would take her to work it out. 'Yes, we did,' she replied softly. 'And he's been wonderful with the children this week.'

'Oh, tell me about it. I've been hearing his virtues extolled by all and sundry. And yours. I owe you both a massive thank you—and not just for saving Tom's life.'

'Rubbish,' she said, still plagued by guilt that Tom had become embroiled in someone else's fight but relieved that the conversation had moved on. 'You do know that low-life was after me and Jack? We treated him on Saturday night after what was probably a knife fight and all but handed him to the police on a plate. They didn't have enough to make it stick, though, and he came back looking for us. Made some excuse about his cut hurting, apparently, hoping to run into us, but unfortunately it was Tom.'

Fliss shivered and hugged her knees. 'Well, they've got more than enough to make it stick now. I'm just so glad it hasn't ended up a murder charge. If Jack and Ben hadn't been there…'

She shuddered, and Sally reached out and squeezed her arm. 'Don't. They were, and he's going to be all right. Don't dwell on it.'

'Oh, I try not to, but at night, when I'm lying in our bed all alone and there are six children in the house, all potentially fatherless—it's not so easy to forget that.'

'But he's better now.'

'Oh, yes, he's better, and he should be home next week. He's very fit—since we put the pool in he's been in it every day, summer and winter. Having it enclosed in a retractable canopy has been wonderful for that. And safer, because it's enclosed. And he insisted on the cover on runners that seals the pool completely, so nobody can fall in. He says he's seen too many children brought in drowned from falling into ponds and pools.'

Her eyes swivelled back to Jack, and she said, 'So tell me about you two.'

Sally felt the tension return instantly, and tried to make her voice casual. 'Oh, we're old history.'

'Really?' Fliss said. She sounded sceptical. 'So what happened on the walk last Sunday? One minute you were all getting on fine, the next you could cut the tension between you with a knife.'

Her heart skittered. 'Really? I didn't notice,' she lied, and Fliss snorted.

'Rubbish. It must be difficult conducting an affair in private with the children around—but I suppose you've got the weekends?' she probed carefully.

'So soon after David? Whatever do you think I am?' she flustered, trying to cover herself, but Fliss just laughed softly.

'A woman?' she said, her voice gentle, and Sally felt her eyes fill with tears. 'A woman still in love with the man who gave her her first child?'

She turned to Fliss, her eyes wide with shock, and Fliss smiled wryly. 'I thought so. Oh, Sally. Are you OK?'

'Does everyone know? Oh, lord, are they all talking about it?'

Fliss laughed. 'I have no idea what they're all talking about, I've been sitting at Tom's bedside, but, no, I don't think they all know, and I've only just guessed. I was watching them from the bedroom window a minute ago, and they're just so alike I can't believe I didn't see it at the wedding.'

'You weren't expecting it.'

'No.' She reached out a hand and touched Sally gently. 'Does Jack know?'

She nodded wordlessly.

'So are you OK? And how's David with it?'

She rubbed her arms briskly for something to do. 'He's been fine. Worried for me, worried for Alex, but he's always known there'd come a time when Alex would have to find out.'

'Does he know?' Fliss asked, her voice shocked, but Sally shook her head hastily.

'No—absolutely not, and we don't want him to. Not yet. Not until the time's right.'

'And when will that be?' Fliss asked thoughtfully. 'Gosh, how hard for you all. Sally, if there's anything I can do to help…?'

'No, we're fine. For now. If there ever is a time, maybe you could have Ben over, invent some excuse so they can be alone and get to know each other.'

'Of course. Just say the word. Right, time to get this lot into bed and then I can slip back and say goodnight to my husband. And Catherine's home, so why don't you take a bottle of wine and go up to the flat with Jack and spend some time together? The kids'll be fine for a little while, and you look as if you could use some down-time. Jack does, anyway. He must be exhausted.'

Down-time? With Jack?

Oh, what a wonderfully tempting thought. Time just to be together, after all the stress and trauma of the week, with Tom hugely improved and out of the woods and her fear for their lives retreating to a manageable level.

She wasn't sure about the wine, though. It had been less than a fortnight since she'd sworn she'd never drink another drop, and here she was, on her second drink this evening. Although, to be fair, she was wearing most of that one.

Fliss hailed Jack and the boys, sent Michael up into the tree-house to bring the girls down and suggested a shower.

The girls were keen enough, but the boys looked unimpressed—until Jack said, 'I tell you what, Sal. Why don't you take the girls and I'll take the boys? And Fliss can sort out towels and PJs and file them all in the right beds, and we'll have a race to see which team gets finished first.'

'Us!' the boys yelled, heading for the house, and the girls ran after them, with the adults trailing a useless third.

'You and your good ideas,' Fliss said, laughing, but between them they had all the children showered, teeth cleaned and into bed within ten minutes. The girls' hair hadn't been washed, but Harriet didn't seem to care and Abby was only too glad to be at home with her father on the mend and was happy to do anything she was asked, so she hadn't presented any problems.

Then she heard Jack's low, rumbling voice as he read the boys a story. 'I haven't heard this book before,' she said to Fliss, but Fliss shook her head.

'He doesn't read them, he makes them up. He's brilliant. He'd be a really good father.' That last so softly that only Sally, standing right beside her, could hear.

Oh, if only. She felt her heart hitch and, telling herself not to be a sentimental fool, she found a book in the bookcase and sent Fliss off to see her beloved Tom, then snuggled down with the girls and read to them.

When she looked up Jack was standing in the doorway, his eyes gentle on her, and she gave him a smile, finished the book and then kissed both girls goodnight before heading for the stairs after him.

'Fliss has left us a bottle of wine and instructions to drink it in my flat,' he murmured, and she felt heat flow through her like melted chocolate, warm and sweet—and addictive.

'Is that a good idea?'

His smile was wry. 'Probably not, but it's a great one.'

So they took the bottle and went up to the little flat over

the kitchen, and there in the privacy of his sitting room they sat down on the sofa, snuggled up together and sipped the wine.

'Australian. It's a good one,' he said, studying the label when he topped the glasses up. 'Nice.'

He put the bottle down, then glanced at her, took the glass from her hand and put it down on the table next to the bottle and drew her into his arms.

'Jack, we can't!' she protested, but he just kissed her lightly and shook his head.

'It's OK. I'm not going to make love to you. I just want to hold you.'

So she relaxed against him, letting him kiss her, his lips trailing over her face, her eyes, her cheeks, down the side of her neck, back up over her chin to her mouth, then brushing lightly over her lips until she opened to him.

After a while he lifted his head, brushed her hair gently off her face and sighed. 'Do you know we've never done this? Just sat together? We've worked together, and we've slept together, and we've made love in every known position, but we've never just sat together quietly and talked.'

'What do you want to talk about?' she asked, and his mouth twisted a little.

'My son?' he said softly. 'He's such a great kid. And he's really nice to his little brother. As a little brother, I can appreciate that.'

She laughed. 'He isn't always nice to him.'

'Oh, of course not, that wouldn't be human, but by and large he seems to be. The only time I've seen him lose it was when Ben put an earwig in his drink.'

She laughed again. 'Sounds like Ben. He can't understand that not everybody likes bugs.'

They fell silent for a while, and then Jack said quietly, 'Is he going to hate me when he knows I'm his father?'

She turned her head. 'Hate you? Why should he hate you?'

'Because I wasn't around?'

'No. He'll hate me, if anyone, because I didn't tell you, but Alex isn't a person who hates. He'll just want to love you, too.'

Jack's face twisted, and he turned away, his jaw working.

'I need to tell him, Sal,' he said gruffly. 'I need him to know, because I love him already, and I can't imagine loving him any more if I'd known him all his life. I watched all those videos. Some of them didn't make much sense, but it didn't matter. It was just seeing him. Watching him grow up. Without me.' He shook his head. 'I don't want that happening any more.'

She felt panic rising in her chest. 'Jack, we can't rush him. Let me talk to David. We need to do this right.'

His eyes were sad. 'Is there ever going to be a right way to tell a little boy that the man he's known as his father isn't his father, and a total stranger is? I don't think so.'

She closed her eyes.

He was right. There was never going to be an easy way to do it, but right then she couldn't see any way at all.

CHAPTER TEN

HE'D promised he'd give her time and he'd meant it, but every moment of it was bitter-sweet.

They had a great day on Sunday in and around the Whittakers' pool, and he discovered that his son—his son, for goodness' sake, that was so hard to get used to!—was a natural swimmer, as he had been. They'd played and wrestled in the water, Alex determined to get the ball off him, and when he'd eventually done it, his cocky pride was one hundred per cent familiar. Jack had to admit to feeling a matching pride for him, but the physical contact with the boy's lithe, muscular young body was curiously painful.

He'd been nine years too late to hold him at birth, to feel his strength grow, to watch the first wobbly efforts at holding his head up, the first time he'd rolled over, the first shaky step. And now Alex was fit and athletic and growing like a weed, and Jack had an overwhelming urge to protect him from any harm that might befall him. He just wanted to take him in his arms and hug him, to have the right to do so, the right to tell him how much he was growing to love him.

He was hugely conscious, though, of not singling Alex out for more than his share of attention and, in fact, Ben in his very different way was just as delightful. He was like Sal, mischievous and full of fun, and yet curiously studious. Fixated on anything small and creepy, of course, and Jack thought that if the budding entomologist went into a career in some sort of biological science, he wouldn't be surprised.

And the Whittaker kids were great, too, and at one point he ended up with the littlest on his lap, just over a year old and utterly enchanting, if a bit wriggly. He wanted to get down, to go and do things, and Jack ended up walking round the garden with him, holding him by the fingers and showing him things.

He handed him back, though, when the nappy needed attention. He wasn't that great with other people's kids! Besides, that meant taking him inside, out of sight and sound of Sal and her boys—the people he was fast beginning to think of as his family.

When she took the children home at the end of the day, he went with her, stayed for supper and then dropped in on Tom on the way back. It had been a day or two since he'd seen him, and he wanted to check up on his patient, friend and colleague.

Jack found him propped up against the pillows, his colour considerably better than the last time he'd seen him, and he greeted Jack with a smile.

'Well, if it isn't my saviour,' he murmured, and moved the newspaper so Jack could sit down.

'How are you?'

'Bloody sore. You could have made a smaller incision.'

Jack laughed, glad to see he was recovering his sense of humour. 'No way. Sorry. There wasn't time to fairy about with keyhole surgery.'

'I've noticed,' Tom said drily. 'Every time I move.'

Jack winced and apologised again, this time with feeling, but Tom just shook his head, his face taut with emotion.

'Don't apologise,' he said gruffly. 'I've got six kids, and thanks to you I might get to see them all grow up and graduate and get married. I can't tell you what that means.'

'You don't need to,' Jack replied, just as gruffly. The thought of missing the rest of Alex's life was too hard to contemplate.

Tom tipped his head on one side and studied him for a moment, then said softly, 'Fliss is right, he is like you.'

His jaw dropped and he hauled it back up. 'Pardon?'

'OK, if that's the way you want to play it, we'll pretend we don't know.'

Don't know? That took a moment to get used to, but Tom just lay there watching him, waiting, and after a moment Jack sighed.

'Is it going to be a problem for you?'

'What—that Alex is yours? Why should it?'

Jack shrugged. 'Patrick had a problem at first, but he's OK now. He's appointed himself Sal's champion.'

'Oh. He giving you a hard time?'

'He has done—for all the right reasons—but I don't think he trusted me to do the decent thing. He's OK now, though, but don't forget, we go back years. He's like a brother, and brothers can get a bit heavy.'

'Well, I won't,' Tom said easily. 'I think you and Sally are great together. You think alike, you don't have to talk—I was like that with Fliss. You can tell a lot from working with a person, and we just clicked. I think you two are the same.'

'We are—at work. It remains to be seen if we are in our private lives—but, then, the chance to have one would be good.'

Tom snorted and rested his head back. 'Take advantage of the flat, if you want. We aren't going to judge you, but you'd be amazed how you can manage to work around the kids. How do you think we ended up with two more? I was going to have a vasectomy, but oddly I don't fancy any more surgery just at the moment.'

'Funny, that,' Jack said with a grin, and then for the first time gave some thought to the question of birth control. It hadn't even occurred to him that he could get Sal pregnant, but he'd rather assumed she had some kind of contraceptive regime in place, as she'd been until so recently a married woman.

But what if she didn't? What if they'd both just overlooked it?

'So tell me,' Tom asked quietly. 'What exactly did that little bastard do to me?'

Jack forced himself to focus. 'He was very tidy, actually. The blade went into the fifth intercostal space, and nicked your pulmonary artery.'

'How close to my heart?'

He shook his head. 'You don't want to know.'

'Yes, I do.'

'He shaved the pericardium.'

'So—close, then. Did I have a massive haemothorax?'

'No. You were hosing blood.'

Tom managed to laugh—just about. 'Right. OK. Well, I suppose I asked. What about my lung?'

'Remarkably little damage. You'd get worse from a broken rib.'

Tom nodded thoughtfully and closed his eyes, and Jack stood up. 'You're looking bushed. I'm going home. Well, to your home, I suppose.'

'Give it my love,' he said wearily. 'I can't wait to get back there. It's so noisy in here.'

Jack laughed and patted his shoulder. 'You stay here as long as you can. It was a riot there today.'

'But it's a different sort of noise. It's kids being happy. I can do that. I just want to be home.'

Jack could understand that. He was looking forward to getting home himself.

Or the nearest thing he had to a home these days.

He'd moved into the Whittakers' flat partly because of being there to help Fliss out and partly because he'd felt he'd been in the way at Patrick and Annie's. Not only that, with Sal and Annie being such close friends, there was a bit of a conflict of interests there, and as he'd said to Tom, Patrick didn't seem to trust him to take care of Sal, and that hurt.

Not that they weren't doing it for all the right reasons, and he loved them for caring so much about her, but he found having to justify his every breath a bit like hard work and it was great to be able to kick off his shoes, put his feet up on the coffee-table and watch what he wanted on the television.

Of course, if he was going to be around for long, he ought to look for a proper place to stay—rent a house or something—just until he'd resolved how this was going to work with Sally.

And if he was lucky—well, he didn't like to think about that too much, not at this stage, because it seemed like tempting fate. He knew what he wanted, but getting it was a whole different ball game, and he had a feeling it could easily end in a no-score draw.

He walked out of the surgical unit and straight into Patrick. 'Talk of the devil,' he said lightly. 'I was just telling Tom you've been giving me a hard time.'

Patrick's eyes shadowed with distress. 'I have, haven't I? Annie gave me an earful this morning about it. I'm sorry. I was busy thinking about Sally, and I totally lost sight of what you must be going through.'

Jack nodded, looking down, kicking the floor gently with his toe. 'It's the fact that you don't trust me to look after her that hurts,' he said, his voice suddenly choked, and with a muttered curse Patrick reached out and squeezed his shoulder hard.

'I'm sorry. You must be going through hell, and I didn't even think of your side. Does he know yet?'

'No, but we'll get there,' he said. 'Somehow.' He swallowed hard and kicked the floor again. Damn. He wasn't going to cry.

'If there's anything we can do…'

'I'll let you know.'

'And you didn't have to move out, you know. You're always welcome. You can come back at any time.'

He looked up and gave his friend a wry smile. 'It's OK. I think I'm going to find a bigger place anyway once Tom comes home—somewhere I can have the boys to stay maybe.'

Patrick cocked his head on one side and frowned. 'But—I thought you wanted to be with Sally?'

He gave a strangled laugh. 'Oh, I do—but what I want and what I'll get may not be the same thing, and I'm not banking on it. Life's taught me not to take anything for granted.'

'Lord, you have grown up.'

Jack smiled. 'It was about time.'

'Welcome back!'

'Really? Tom's at death's door, Al's wandering around

with his hand in a support, about as much use as a chocolate teapot, and you reckon I'm welcome?' Matt Jordan snorted softly, and Sally shook her head and hugged the big Canadian.

'It's good to see you.'

'Ditto.' He stood back and looked at her, his head cocked on one side. 'Look, I'm sorry about you and David.'

'Ah. You heard.'

'I did—Tom told me last week, before he got himself stabbed. So are you OK?'

'I'm fine,' she said, not sure whether it was true or not. Bit of a curate's egg—good in parts. That would have been the honest answer. 'Um—we've got a locum, by the way, so it's not as grim as it could be.'

'Yeah, Jack Logan. I heard about him from Tom as well. Patrick's best man. He was a lucky find—and I gather he's an old friend of yours?'

'Um, yes,' she began, but just then Jack strolled round the corner, stethoscope slung round his neck, cuffs turned back to show off his tanned, hair-strewn wrists, and she couldn't stop her smile. Matt raised an eyebrow and chuckled softly.

'Your friend, huh? OK.' He held out his hand and raised his voice a little. 'You must be Jack. I'm Matt.'

'Hi. Good to meet you. Morning, gorgeous.'

'Morning,' she said, trying to squash the smile, but she could do nothing about the touch of colour that warmed her cheeks, and Matt missed nothing. Damn. 'I'll leave you two to get to know each other,' she said, and made herself walk away.

She didn't want to. She wanted to stay with Jack.

For the rest of her life, if she was honest, but it was too

soon, and she had to sort out the children first. And be utterly certain of his motives.

She found Angie, still wearing an ankle support but much better now a week down the road, and begged for Triage. Nice and busy, and away from Jack, but Angie shook her head.

'I thought I'd do it. Had a bit of a silly weekend in the garden as it was so gorgeous, and my ankle's playing up. Do you mind? You can choose cubicles or majors.'

On Monday morning? She chose majors. Cubicles would be nothing but sunburn and hayfever and sporting injuries from the weekend. At least majors might be interesting.

Obviously it wasn't only her mind that worked that way, because when she went to meet the first ambulance that came in, Jack was at her side.

'You've caught the sun,' he said, smiling at her. 'You look positively healthy.'

'You mean my nose is red.'

'No, I mean you look beautiful,' he replied softly, and turned his attention to the ambulance that was backing up to the doors. 'I wonder if this one's got cataplexy.'

'Well, you're just lucky I'm here with you,' she said lightly, and his smile was gentle.

'Oh, don't I know it,' he murmured.

Then the doors opened, and all hell broke loose.

It was a busy day—the start of a busy week—and Sally found herself rushing around both at work and at home. She had Abby and Michael again on Tuesday, and while Ben took Abby down the garden and showed her an earwig's nest, Michael and Alex went into the study and did some research on the internet for Alex's homework.

They were in there for ages, and she stuck her head

round the door at one point and found they weren't even looking at the screen.

'Hey, come on, you two, if you've finished come out of there and go in the garden. It's a lovely evening and it seems a shame to be shut up inside.'

They came, but from then on Alex seemed unusually quiet.

That troubled her, when she had time to think about it. Why? What had they found on the internet?

Porn?

She felt cold at the thought. Surely not? They were far too young to be thinking about things like that. On Thursday evening, when Alex was still a little withdrawn, she went into the study and checked the log on the computer to see which sites they'd been accessing, and found nothing dubious at all.

They could have picked up a link, she thought, but there was no evidence, so she shut the computer down and was just about to leave the room when the phone rang.

'Sally, it's me,' David said. 'I've had a thing through from the court and they want information I haven't got. You might find it in the filing cabinet, in the file with all the birth certificates and things.'

She turned towards the filing cabinet and then noticed the file was lying on the desk. 'Oh—I've got it. We must have left it out last week. What did you want to know?'

She didn't hear his answer. She didn't hear or see anything except the roaring in her ears, because there, lying on the top where they most certainly hadn't left it, was Alex's birth certificate, with Ben's right underneath. They were both out of the envelopes, both open, shoved hastily back into the pocket folder.

'David, I think we've got a problem,' she said, nausea

rising in her throat. 'Did you leave the children's birth certificates out of their envelopes in the top of the folder?'

'No. We looked at them for the information, then put them away. Why?'

'Because they're out and at the top. I think when Alex and Michael were in here checking something on the internet, they may have looked at them.'

David swore softly. 'Want me to come over?'

'Maybe. I don't know. But I think we're going to have to tell him soon. Maybe even tonight, but I'd rather leave it till the weekend when we've all got more time to talk.'

She saw Jack drawing up outside and waved to him through the window. 'Look, Jack's here. I'll tell him about this, and we'll see if Alex says anything. I might be jumping to conclusions, but he's been a bit quiet all week.'

'Call me if you need me. You know I'll come.'

'OK.'

She shut the folder, went to the front door and outside, hugging her arms, although it was far from cold.

Jack shut the car door and turned to her with a grin, bouncing a new football on his foot, but one look at her face and his grin faded, the ball rolling forgotten into the flower-bed.

'What is it?'

'I think he knows David isn't his father.'

Jack felt a chill run through him. Sal quickly filled him in about her suspicions, and he closed his eyes, trying to slow his thundering heart.

'So this is it?'

'Could be. Come on, I don't want to talk outside, but I wanted to warn you. We'll go into the kitchen.'

She led him in, and Ben came running up, grinning, and hugged Jack round the waist. 'Hiya!' he said cheerfully, and Jack put an arm round his shoulders and hugged him back.

'Hiya, young 'un. You all right?'

'Mmm. There's an earwig nest—come and see.'

'Later. I could do with a drink, and your mum and I need to have a talk.'

'Work again?' Ben said, wrinkling his nose, and Jack gave him a grin that felt slightly off-kilter and nodded. He ran off, and she shut the door and turned to Jack.

'We have to do this,' she said. 'I know it's time, but—how? There are so many unknowns. He'll need to see you, and you'll need to see him, but God knows where you'll be—'

'Here,' he cut in. 'I'll be right here.'

'For ever? What about work commitments? You can't be sure. And he needs to know, needs to have some certainty. I mean, already for birthdays and Christmas and things he's going to be split two ways. I don't think I can cope with it being three.'

She broke off, tears spilling down her cheeks, and he tried to hold her but she turned away, swiping the tears from her face and pulling herself together visibly. 'Don't touch me, Jack. I can hardly—'

'It doesn't need to be three,' he said, gripping the back of a chair to stop him from reaching for her. 'I've been thinking. It was something Tom said the other day about having a vasectomy because they'd got so many kids, and I suddenly thought, I know it hasn't been many times, but we haven't used any contraception, and I don't know if we needed to, but if we did needed to and we didn't, and there's a baby, how would I feel? And the answer is over-joyed, because I can't think of anything I want more than to have children with you—your boys and any others that come along.

'And it's not just to be with Alex. I know he's my son, and I know at some point we're going to have to deal with this, but at the bottom of it all is the fact that I love you, that I've always loved you, that I've never stopped loving you, and I should have been with you for the last ten years. And I know it's difficult, and I don't want to rush things because the boys have only just lost David, but I love them already, Sal. And I love you. And I can't walk away from this—not this time.'

His eyes filled, and he broke off and blinked. 'Don't ask me to go. I can't. I've missed nine years of Alex's life, and ten years of ours, and I don't want to miss another minute.'

His voice cracked, and she turned to him.

'So what are you suggesting?' she asked warily.

'Marriage—what else? I'm asking you to marry me, Sal. Come live with me and be my love. And the rest will sort itself out, because all of us love the children. I know Alex is mine and so he's somehow closer to my heart, but Ben's so like you, and such a great kid, how could I not love him, too?'

'And David?'

'David's Alex's dad. I know that, my love. He always will be. He's the man who brought him up, the man he's called his father. I wouldn't expect either of them to give that up. I know how it feels. I'll never get over losing Chloe to Greg, and I don't think she will. So, no, David doesn't need to feel threatened by my presence in your life, far from it. But I need to be with you, and I need to be with my son.'

His voice cracked again, and he stopped and sucked in air, forcing his breathing to slow. Sal, say something, he pleaded silently, but when the voice came, it wasn't hers, it was Alex's, from behind him, in the doorway.

'Are you my father?'

Oh, lord. He felt the blood drain from his head, felt a cold sweat break out as his heart picked up speed, and he turned and looked his son in the eye while Sal stood there, hand hovering near her mouth, rooted to the spot.

He searched the guarded young face, the vulnerable eyes, the mouth that was set in a grim line, hanging on, and he wanted to weep for him.

'Yes,' he said gruffly. 'I'm your father—your natural father.'

'So why aren't you on my birth certificate? I said if there wasn't anybody on it, then I couldn't have a father, but Michael said that was stupid, everybody has a father, even if they don't live with them. He said maybe Mum didn't know who it was.'

There was a gasp of denial from beside Jack, but he didn't look round. He couldn't take his eyes off his son. 'She knew. She just couldn't tell me, because I'd gone away and she didn't know how to find me. And you can only put it down when the person isn't there if you're married to him. And we weren't married.'

Alex's eyes flicked to his mother. 'Is that true?'

'Yes,' she said unsteadily. 'Yes, it's true.'

'So Dad's not my dad?'

'Yes, he is,' Jack put in swiftly. 'And he always will be, but he's not related to you. There's a difference between a father and a dad. There shouldn't be, in an ideal world, but sometimes there is, and the man who brings you up, who cares for you and loves you and answers all your endless questions and wipes your bottom when you're little and listens to you read and teaches you to ride a bike—that man's your dad. And he always will be.'

'But didn't you want to do that?'

Jack felt the tears scald his cheeks, but there was nothing he could do about it, so he did the next best thing and ignored it. 'Oh, yes,' he said softly. 'I would have given everything to be that man for you, but I didn't know you were alive. If I had, wild horses wouldn't have kept me away from you.'

'You're crying.'

'Because it breaks my heart,' Jack said honestly. And then, fearing rejection but unable to stand the look on his son's face, he opened his arms and waited. 'Come here,' he said softly, and after a moment's hesitation Alex took one step, then another, and then ran into his arms.

Sally couldn't see.

The tears were streaming down her cheeks, Alex was sobbing in Jack's arms, and she didn't think he was hanging on too well either. And then David walked in.

'David,' she said, and Alex lifted his head and turned, and ran to him.

'Dad!' he said, and David swept him up into his arms and hugged him hard without a word.

Then Ben wandered in, took one look at them all and dropped the beetle in his hand. 'What's going on?'

Jack just looked at her, and she went over to him, to the man she loved, slipped her hand into his and said, 'Jack's just asked me to marry him, and I've said yes.'

'You have?' Jack said, hope dawning in his eyes, and

then with a ragged laugh he hauled her into his arms and crushed her to his chest. 'Oh, thank you,' he whispered unsteadily, and she hugged him back.

'Don't thank me,' she said. 'I'm only doing what I've wanted all along—being with the man I love.'

She let him go and went over to David, standing now with Alex beside him, and she put her arms around him and hugged him, too. 'I'm sorry. I never should have married you, it wasn't fair, but you've been fantastic, and if I hadn't Ben wouldn't be here, and I can't imagine the world without him, and you've been the best father the boys could have wished for, but I just want to be happy, like you are with Wendy.'

'That's all I want for you, too,' he said, hugging her hard, and then he turned her and pushed her back towards Jack. 'Come on, boys, let's leave them to it. I expect they want to do soppy stuff.'

'Oh, yuck,' Ben said, but Alex gave Jack a lingering look, as if he didn't really want to leave him.

'Five minutes,' Jack said. 'Deal?'

Alex nodded. 'Deal.'

They went out and closed the door, and she walked into his arms, rested her head on his chest and sighed.

His voice rumbled under her ear. 'Did you really mean it?'

'Mean what?' she asked, tipping her head back so she could see him.

'That you'll marry me.'

'Of course I meant it.'

'It wasn't just for the boys' benefit?'

She straightened away from him, staring at him in consternation. 'Of course not. Jack, I love you. I've always loved you, but you've never said it to me and so I never said it back. I thought…'

She broke off, and he tipped his head on one side. 'You thought…?'

She shrugged. 'Maybe it was just sex. Maybe it was just convenient—and then you found out about Alex and you thought, Why not? Good sex and you get to see your son—'

'Hey, hang on. I'm not that bothered about sex.'

'That's ridiculous! You make love to me so often when we're together—'

'Because I want you. You. Not sex. I want to be with you, to hold you, to touch you. To be close to you. It's only you that does that to me. Nothing else has ever come close. And it's because I love you.'

Her eyes filled, and she rested her head back against his chest. 'I'm so glad because, now I think about it, you might be right. About the contraception.'

He went still, then shifted so he could see her face. 'Meaning?'

'I think—I've been feeling queasy this week, but I thought it was knowing we'd got to tell Alex. It might not have been.'

Joy lit his eyes, and with a ragged sigh he gathered her gently against his heart.

'Oh, my darling girl,' he breathed, and pressed his lips to her forehead. She tilted her face up, and his lips found hers, and it was like no other kiss he'd ever given her.

It was a kiss of affirmation, of promise, of thanks.

A kiss of love.

And then the door opened, and a voice said, 'We had a deal. Five minutes.'

Jack laughed softly against Sally's mouth and lifted his head.

'I'm coming, son,' he said.

* * *

'A girl?'

Jack grinned and hugged the boys.

'That's the one.'

'Can we see her?'

'Sure. Come on up.'

He led them through the garden door of their pretty but not-so-little Victorian house, the stuff of Sal's dreams, and up the stairs to their bedroom. The midwife was still busy in the background, but Sally—his beautiful, clever, beloved wife—was lying there, propped up in bed with the baby at her breast, looking utterly sublime. His daughter was still streaked with blood, but one little starfish hand was pressed to the pale, blue-veined skin of Sally's breast, and her rosebud mouth was working noisily.

'Wow,' Alex said softly. 'She's so tiny. Can I touch her?'

'Of course you can,' Sally said, smiling at him. He slid his finger under the tiny hand and she gripped it, and he grinned.

'Hey, she's really strong!'

'She's cool—bit messy, but she's cute,' Ben chipped in, going round the other side and climbing up onto the bed for a better look. He sat down on the pillow and put his head on his mother's shoulder and watched his little sister feed, while Alex stood there with his finger in her tiny hand, and Jack thought his heart would burst.

'I wonder what Wendy's having?' Ben said.

'I reckon a boy,' Alex answered. 'Meg had a girl, then Annie had a boy, and Mum's had a girl, and so it's their turn for a boy.'

'Does it matter?' Sally asked, and they both shook their heads.

'No. They all cry all night,' Ben said sagely, and Jack met his wife's eyes and laughed.

'Oh, joy, I can hardly wait,' he said, and he meant every word...

0407/03a

MILLS & BOON®

_MedicaL
romance™

A BRIDE FOR GLENMORE
by Sarah Morgan

GP Ethan Walker arrives on the remote Scottish
island of Glenmore to spend one summer – and one
summer only – as a locum at the island's surgery.
Ethan can't reveal his real reason for being on the
island, and although his head tells him he should stay
away from beautiful practice nurse Kyla MacNeil, he
is unable to resist their attraction...

A MARRIAGE MEANT TO BE
by Josie Metcalfe

Con and Callie Lowell have the perfect marriage
– or so it seems. In reality, years of failed IVF
treatment has left them heartbroken and distant.
Callie believes Con wants a woman who can give
him a child, so she flees – leaving behind nothing but
a note and a bewildered husband... Can Con track
her down and convince her their marriage is meant
to be?

DR CONSTANTINE'S BRIDE
by Jennifer Taylor

Nurse Katie Carlyon has come to start a new life
in the Cypriot sunshine, where her nursing skills
– and vulnerable beauty – instantly impress the man
sent to meet her: handsome A&E doctor Christos
Constantine. Christos is quick to offer Katie a job
and as they work together sparks begin to fly...

On sale 4th May 2007

Available at WHSmith, Tesco, ASDA, and all good bookshops

www.millsandboon.co.uk

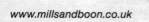

4 FREE

BOOKS AND A SURPRISE GIFT!

We would like to take this opportunity to thank you for reading this Mills & Boon® book by offering you the chance to take FOUR more specially selected titles from the Medical Romance™ series absolutely FREE! We're also making this offer to introduce you to the benefits of the Mills & Boon® Reader Service™—

- ★ **FREE home delivery**
- ★ **FREE gifts and competitions**
- ★ **FREE monthly Newsletter**
- ★ **Exclusive Reader Service offers**
- ★ **Books available before they're in the shops**

Accepting these FREE books and gift places you under no obligation to buy, you may cancel at any time, even after receiving your free shipment. Simply complete your details below and return the entire page to the address below. You don't even need a stamp!

YES! Please send me 4 free Medical Romance books and a surprise gift. I understand that unless you hear from me, I will receive 6 superb new titles every month for just £2.89 each, postage and packing free. I am under no obligation to purchase any books and may cancel my subscription at any time. The free books and gift will be mine to keep in any case.

M7ZED

Ms/Mrs/Miss/Mr .... Initials ....

BLOCK CAPITALS PLEASE

Surname ....

Address ....

....

.... Postcode ....

Send this whole page to:
UK: FREEPOST CN81, Croydon, CR9 3WZ